The Molehill

Malicious Conspiracy of International Intrigue, Betrayal, Mayhem and Murder

Kurt Hafner

authorHOUSE

AuthorHouse™ UK
1663 Liberty Drive
Bloomington, IN 47403 USA
www.authorhouse.co.uk
Phone: UK TFN: 0800 0148641 (Toll Free inside the UK)
UK Local: (02) 0369 56322 (+44 20 3695 6322 from outside the UK)

© 2023 Kurt Hafner. All rights reserved.

No part of this book may be reproduced, stored in a retrieval system, or transmitted by any means without the written permission of the author.

Published by AuthorHouse 12/05/2023

ISBN: 979-8-8230-8490-1 (sc)
ISBN: 979-8-8230-8491-8 (hc)
ISBN: 979-8-8230-8489-5 (e)

Print information available on the last page.

Any people depicted in stock imagery provided by Getty Images are models, and such images are being used for illustrative purposes only.
Certain stock imagery © Getty Images.

This book is printed on acid-free paper.

Because of the dynamic nature of the Internet, any web addresses or links contained in this book may have changed since publication and may no longer be valid. The views expressed in this work are solely those of the author and do not necessarily reflect the views of the publisher, and the publisher hereby disclaims any responsibility for them.

Synopsis

The 'Molehill' is a dramatic international thriller and the sequel to 'Spider's Web' with many of the favourite characters plus newcomers continuing their fight against organized crime, vile threats, intrigue, and betrayal.

Rolf and Sabine Brenner's flourishing business in UK, Germany, Switzerland and the United States comes under attack once more after several years of peace and quiet following what had come to be known as 'The Spider's Web Incident'.

A predator, Milton Adams is the mysterious owner of an enormous business empire which had grown through his ruthless tactics of subversive activities, bribery, intimidation, threats, strong arm tactics and murder.

His new head quarter is located in a remote valley in the Central Swiss mountains which can only be reached through secret passages and caves. Milton calls his giant fortified chalet 'The Earie' due to the way that he compares himself with an Eagle soaring way above in the sky, watching his prey, ready to swoop with his talons out to grab whatever he desires.

Rolf and Sabine Brenner's organization in England, Germany, Switzerland and the United States are on Milton's radar and his ruthless tactics soon result in murder, mayhem and destruction. A secret cross bow assassin, a flight attendant in mortal danger further add to a kaleidoscope of the unfolding drama.

The actions zigzag between Switzerland, Germany, England, Italy, Florida, New York and Colorado and ultimately culminate in a dramatic, explosive conclusion to the Molehill incident.

Reflections about The Author

Having 'sneaked' an initial copy of 'The Molehill' I immediately found myself engrossed in intrigue, launched in the centre of the Swiss Alps, speedily moving on, via leafy Hampshire, to a criminal environment in Hamburg – then via London Heathrow Airport on to Denver and Southwest Florida. From there, back to the UK and then, by Concorde to New York and Manhattan. Returning once again to Europe, to Bologna Italy and finally back once more to the US, to Colorado!

Phew, what a whirlwind kaleidoscope of locations and subsequent events all accurately and lovingly described!

Add to this a plethora of different characters, ranging from young business entrepreneurs to a predatory villain, The Swiss Secret Service, British Intelligence, a young female military commander, a Norlands Nanny, a sinister Monk, characters in mortal danger including an airline Flight Attendant, the individual thoughts and feelings of the various characters … … all leading to a very 'Explosive' conclusion to a brilliant story.

Now to the big question….**Am I surprised** …. **not in the least!**

Having known Kurt Hafner for over 50 years I have long come to 'expect the unexpected', a sense of positivity like no other, creativity and 'bucket loads' of surprises! But then when one considers his Swiss ancestry with his Mother's side abounding in pride with a background of Head Masters, Teachers, Authors, Philosophers, Broadcasters and Journalists and, his Father's side Nationally known Hotel Owners, International experts in Hospitality, Culinary expertise, and a nationally known Professor of Zoology 'to boot', it is hardly surprising!

Kurt's description of Countries, locations, of people's feelings and characteristics in five languages, of food and beverages are a true reflection of his love of people, his sense of adventure and his international global experience which leaves little need for consideration of my question ... Am I surprised?

Enjoy this masterpiece and, as you do, reflect on its many elements of experience and authenticity, as indeed have I.

Mike (or Michael if you prefer) Street OBE

About this book

All the many personalities and characters featured in this book are completely fictional and bare no relationship to any living person or those previously alive either in the United Kingdom or abroad.

A background of operating on a global basis has provided me with the pleasure and experience of enjoying the service of premium companies, top quality brands and their people at many different levels which I have great pleasure to positively reflect in this novel with my thanks and compliments on their degree of excellence.

However all the involvement of these organisations, brands and their people in whatever capacity in this novel are complete inventions, pure creations and complete fictions of my imagination.

Dedication

This sequel to 'Spider's Web' is dedicated to my lovely wife Mary, who's patience, sparkling personality and support, allowed me to enter my world of mystery and fantasy.

At the same time it is also dedicated to our three daughters: -

Clare
Emma
Mary-Anne

Whose lively families, ideas, support and creativity have encouraged me to escape into my realm of magic, mystery and surprise.

Finally it is my great pleasure to pay a massive tribute to Sanibel Beach Club II, where all of us have enjoyed our three weeks for over 25 years and where 'Spider's web' was created with this wonderful resort featured in many chapters of the book and its sequel 'The Molehill.

Calendar of Events

Chapter Number	Title	Location
1	The Secret Valley	Switzerland
2	Rolf Brenner Ltd	Hampshire, England
3	Narrow Escape	Northern Germany
4	Betrayal	Switzerland
5	The Attack	Switzerland
6	War Council	Northern Italy
7	London Heathrow T4	Heathrow, England
8	Investigations	Switzerland
9	The Studio	Queens, New York
10	Central Park South	New York
11	The Delivery	Southwest Florida
12	Interstate 678	New York
13	The Task	Queens, New York
14	Early Dawn	Southwest Florida
15	Flight Encounters	North Atlantic

16	Conspiracy	Switzerland – Italy
17	Boulder	Colorado
18	Retribution	Southwest Florida
19	The Monastery	Switzerland - Italy
20	Exposures	Switzerland – Italy
21	Into The Wilderness	Colorado
22	The Swiss Connection	Switzerland
23	Red Alert	Colorado – New York
24	The Cherokee Solution	High Planes, Colorado
25	The Termination	Northern Italy
26	Breaking News	International Media

The Cast In Order of Appearance

Name	Description
Colonel Peter Burki	Head of the Swiss Secret Service
Rolf Brenner	Owner and Managing Director of Rolf Brenner Ltd. And USA Subsidiaries
Sabine Brenner	Co-Owner and Managing Director of Rolf Brenner Ltd. And USA Subsidiaries
Lord Nigel Britton	Aristocrat, Commercial Genius and creative Entrepreneur
Fenella Hardwick	Glamorous, celebrated lawyer with an outstanding record of defeating predatory criminal elements.
Johann Albrecht	Petty criminal, then sailor, smuggler and now resourceful gang leader.
Hannah Gerber	Attractive, athletic and combative woman in her late thirties and Section Chief of a mysterious new organization.
Colonel Tarrant	Criminal manipulator and imposter, having escaped prosecution for alleged murder and extortion.
Milton Brown	Powerful and secretive manipulator of immense wealth and shady activities.

Musgrove	Sinister Chief of Milton Brown's Operation
Commander Belinda Carrington	Cheltenham educated, Sandhurst graduate, SAS trained British Intelligence Commander, previously seconded to the Swiss Secret Service
Brother Anselmo	Sinister, ambitious and ruthless monk
Christopher Huntingdon	Secretive American, middle aged business executive
Elna Petroni	Attractive and assertive young woman who works in conjunction with Huntingdon
Professor Duncan Cameron	Renowned Professor of modern and historical criminology
Gaston Bleriot	Opinionated, arrogant Frenchman
Professor Tobias Berger	Renowned Professor and authority of Swiss criminal, intelligence
Ueli Amberg	Young farmer managing his parent's estate and lifestock
Pia Marinello	Lively, happy and successful flight attendant for the national airline
Anton Gruber	Resourceful, inquisitive, cunning porter at Pia Marinello's apartment and business complex
Maya Von Gunten	Pia Marinello's devious cousin, secretive housekeeper with sinister motives, during the flight attendant's absence
Valentino Cuccione	Italian Immigrant to the United States successful waiter and amateur painter.
Maria Costello	Fenella Hardwick's PA, trainer and minder

Sergeant Ray Kenny	Promising young NYPD sergeant of Irish origin earmarked for fast track promotion.
Sergeant Lara Pregovsky	Sparkling, enthusiastic young police sergeant with a strong background of defeating organized criminals.
Lieutenant Leroy Simmons	Young successful NYPD Lieutenant of detectives, combating organized crime.
Samantha Masterson	Experienced Norland Nannie, in her late twenties employed by Sabine and Rolf Brenner to look after their children.
Edward Pregowsky	Famous retired Commisioner of police
Selina Nelson	Energetic Princeton graduate athlete
Joyce Allan	Recently promoted South West Florida chief of Police
Brad Coulter	USA based senior M15 agent
Arlene Wilson	Attractive, ambitious and assertive waitress with subversive connections
Professor Duncan Cameron	Internationally renowned professor of criminology
Fiona Campbell	Feisty, energetic, Scottish beauty with great memories of her and Belinda's imprisonment and fight to escape a couple of years ago

Chapter 1

The Secret Valley: Switzerland

The peace of the late afternoon was shattered as the thunder of another avalanche reverberated around the valley and the surrounding peaks of the central massive in the heart of the Swiss Mountains.

Sergeant Rita Liechti adjusted her climbing gear and shouted, "Bruno, for heaven's sake stop your playlist; adjust your helmet and microphone pronto."

"All set, Sarge," Corporal Bruno Hintermann saluted and followed his leader towards their dangerous and precarious climb.

Morning had started early for the two Swiss Secret Service officers, following the briefing by Colonel Peter Burki about their mission of reaching the secret observation post and to be in position well before the early rays of the sun painted the distant panorama of snowy peaks in pink for a while.

Their target of observation would be the impressive chalet-style building that dominated the meadow on the other side of the valley. It was perched against the dense pine forest which rose steeply, then made way to the forbidding and overhanging rock face of cliffs, crevices, and gullies reaching to the snowfield and finally the peaks that surrounded this mysterious valley.

They were to identify any suspicious movements, persons, and activities, and note anything unusual of what had been identified as the secret headquarter of an evil organisation and a predatory, ruthless owner of an enormous commercial and criminal empire.

It had turned into a glorious day on the luscious meadow, where a herd of brown cows peacefully grazed. The rustic alp hut, which overlooked the meadow, was adorned by an array of traditional cowbells, ranging from the very large and heavy ones for the lead cows to progressively smaller ones for the heifers and the calves. As the last rays of the sun gradually moved up the hillside, a massive Bernese mountain dog sat at the door of the stable, alert and imperiously surveying his domain.

As they reached the bunker, the view was crystal-clear from the location of the secret lookout. Sergeant Rita was in regular contact with HQ to report any details they noticed at the mysterious building and lavish surroundings on the opposite side of the valley.

Their lookout was ideal and consisted of a bunker that had been constructed in the late thirties as part of the Swiss Army's defences in advance of the sudden start of World War II. The benefit of their observation post was that it was underground, with the exception of the lookout slots, which allowed them to scrutinize any movements within a wide range of vision. Visible recognition was substantially supported by the latest systems of radar, sound recognition, and devices to intercept electronic communications.

Later on, as the shadows grew longer and a calm atmosphere descended onto the valley, Rita asked, "Any news from Armin and Sarah, Bruno?"

"Nothing, ma'am, and yes, they should have arrived by now for a secure handover, well before we start our descent."

"They're late," Rita said.

Bruno shrugged. "You know Armin."

Rita chewed her lip. "Armin, yeah, but Sarah? She's never late."

Bruno put a blade of grass between his lips. "You think perhaps it is sinister?"

"I don't know what to think," Rita said. "I just don't like it."

In the meantime, life across the valley appeared to follow the normal pattern, except there were two black helicopters parked to the right of the building and attended by what appeared to be engineers, flight crew, and other assistants who were loading goods into the choppers.

The Molehill

Rita scanned the top floor of the building and tried to catch a glimpse of any movement happening behind the panoramic windows of the strange chalet that overlooked the valley. She spotted an outline of a tall figure, but even with the most sophisticated electronic devices at her disposal, she was unable to identify any further details, presumably because of the cunning way in which the large panoramic window had been coated.

Just then, Rita called out, "What on earth, Bruno?"

"Yeah, Rita, that dog pulling wheels of cheese on a cart; how mad?"

"And now all the cattle are ready to move. Bruno, report to the colonel; something's afoot."

Colonel Peter Burki was briefing his elite troops about the forthcoming raid. Yes, he would be informed. By the way, they confirmed that Armin and Sarah had left well on time to arrive for the handover and to start their watch on schedule.

"Bruno, watch out, those choppers are ready."

Then an alert, "Yes, Colonel, Bruno is watching them; yes, sir. Certainly, Colonel, we are on the way." She hung up.

"Bruno, action stations; you need to secure all the electronics except the surveillance devices. Colonel wants us to close and lock up immediately, then start our descent. Meet Armin and Sarah Manser for a secure handover. They are on the way but have obviously been delayed; we will probably meet them halfway. So, Bruno, let's move pronto."

"Yes, Sergeant. *Subito*. At your service."

Delays to reaching their location were not unusual, of course, because of the precarious terrain through forest, across an ice field, up a steep incline, and finally through the dangerous rock face including a fierce waterfall and occasional loose boulders.

The two of them quickly and efficiently began closing down all the instruments except for the recording systems and securing all the locking devices on the bunker. Before they finished, they were alerted by commotions that kept them glued to their instruments of observation, until the unthinkable happened.

Chapter 2

Rolf Brenner Limited: Hampshire England

Spring had come early as Rolf and Sabine Brenner were powering along the leafy country lane. It was 0630 on a glorious morning; the sun was just breaking through the trees, and they enjoyed the early chorus of the many birds that populated the lush undergrowth of this forest.

Sabine looked splendid in her designer leggings and fashionable top that accentuated her slim but shapely figure. She felt well and healthy, was bronzed after her holiday in Switzerland, and was already looking forward to the board meeting later that day.

Rolf was also in great shape. He accelerated down a hill, pedalling with increasing energy and enjoying the speed of his specially adapted four-wheel vehicle that had been designed to improve his general mobility after a dreadful accident in Florida eighteen months previously. His initial recovery had been quite miraculous, but thereafter followed many months of fighting the paralysis that had initially crippled him. He was now gradually getting better.

Shortly after his accident, their life was disrupted by a protagonist whose objective was to damage their business, to discredit their share value, and then buy the company and all subsidiaries for a knockdown price. He led a sudden spate of hostile and predatory activities ranging from intimidation, threats, arson, and murder to destroy everything Rolf and Sabine had worked so hard to achieve.

The Molehill

At the same time, Rolf had enlisted the support of personal connections, an international team of experts who had been on the trail of the subversive organization. The combined expertise and resources then brought this episode, which became known as the Spider's Web Incident, to a dramatic and brilliant conclusion.

Thereafter, peace and progress returned to Rolf and Sabine's microelectronics factory and organization, in England and their US subsidiary, Rolf Brenner Inc. Business flourished, the two of them prospered, and the problems that had caused turmoil eighteen months earlier were now well and truly in the past.

As the two of them sped along, Sabine chuckled and said, "Rolf, you cheeky boy, how you pretended to accidentally collide with me in that snowstorm underneath that portal to Waldshut."

"Yeah, Sabi, and you so innocently making googly eyes at me."

"Then as a young teenager, Sabine, when your mother passed away, you immediately took charge of your five brothers and sisters and the task of looking after your father. Clever girl, you soon became a driving force of generating success by motivating the children to achieve excellent grades at school in addition to encouraging your father to progress to a better job and together to turn the fortunes of your family around."

"Aw, great memories, Rolf, and we had such fun spending plenty of time together in between our long hours and intensive schedule, my uni studies for a degree in marketing and your long hours to complete the electronics research project, ready for your return to England."

"Yes, my love, we sure had fun when I declined the lucrative opportunity of joining the Germany company, and you, clever girl, graduated before we both returned to England."

"And here we are now, Rolfi, on our early morning run, taking pride in our highly successful business and our two children; yep, life is good. And now I am getting really hungry."

As the two of them rounded the corner at the end of the forest, their company head office came into view. They were pleased to see the flags had been raised and many cars were already parked around the building.

The design of the factory had been carefully developed to blend into the beautiful countryside of this lush valley in leafy Hampshire and was a source of pride for the two young owners of their specialized electronics business. Rolf's creativity, expertise, and design of the most advanced weapons systems had gained him an unsurpassed reputation.

For this reason, his company had become known as the ultimate place to work, for the brightest and most promising experts and graduates who now formed the core of a brilliant organization. The present therefore looked perfect, and the future appeared to be a period of exciting developments and progress.

As Rolf and Sabine reduced their speed to cool down, they chatted about their plans of returning to southwest Florida the following week for a well-deserved break, combined with their USA business activities, including their subsidiaries in Atlanta and Chicago, in addition to visiting Fenella Hardwick, their lawyer in New York.

When they reached the entrance to the grounds, they were greeted by the two security guards, who opened the electronic gate leading to the attractive and well-tended park land that surrounded the complex of their offices and the factory.

Breakfast was ready in their private suite; they enjoyed it after a refreshing shower and changing into smart casual outfits, then they spent half an hour catching up with the latest general and financial news on TV.

They entered the general offices for a brief update by Helen, their personal assistant, about the current state of play and the program for the coming few days. As they were well prepared for the board meeting and there was sufficient time, they decided to look in on the department heads' meeting, chaired by the general manager of the business.

Around midmorning, a messenger arrived at the security gate and demanded to see Rolf Brenner in person; he had an urgent and personal delivery. The senior security guard asked for identification and details of the motorcyclist's company.

"Wat's it to do wif you, mate?" challenged the courier as he grudgingly showed his driving license and an identity card with photograph, showing him as one Albert Harrison, working for a company listed as CDA.

"Ok, Mr Harrison, that's in order, and if you hand over the package, my colleague will take it to Mr Brenner's office right away," the senior guard said.

The Molehill

"No way, mate," Albert snapped, producing a letter from the ministry of defence, signed by a Colonel McDavish-Brown and confirming the delivery had to be personally handed over to Rolf Brenner.

A telephone call to the executive offices was followed by the second guard escorting Harrison to Rolf and Sabine's personal assistant, who looked up from her desk with a friendly smile and said, "Good morning, what an impressive uniform; my name is Helen. May I please have your name and the company you are working for?"

"Name's Burt, init, an' I work for CDA."

"Well, Albert, it's nice to meet you. May I please take care of the delivery?"'

The courier glowered, stopped her with a raised hand, and growled, "No, love; wat's it wif all of you? It's me bleedin' show, an' I will give this to the boss man meself."

"Well, Albert, if you have to hand it to Mr Brenner personally, then you are welcome to do so, but you will have to wait until the board meeting has finished in about half an hour. My colleague Chloe will take you to the waiting area, where you may help yourself to a cup of coffee or a mineral water."

There was a cunning gleam in Burt's eye as he followed Helen's assistant down the corridor. As he ambled along the passage behind the young lady, he looked at her swaying hips and thought, *Very tasty that, perfect for me.* He then caught up with her and said, "Chloe, this is great, init, and your board room must be real posh."

"Yes, Albert; now here's our waiting area. Please help yourself to a refreshment; there are also some newspapers and magazines over there."

Burt grumbled that there were no newspapers to his liking and the magazines about fashion, horses, and posh idiots were far too boring. But that aside, his mind was clear and sharp, as he looked around and crept back along the corridor to the boardroom.

"Right, Burt, action stations," he said to himself. "I'm bloody well gonna show them what's what." He marched along the corridor and burst through the boardroom door, only being confronted and bumping into a locked inner door. "Shit, bloody hell, poncified outfit," he wanted to shout but wisely muttered under his breath. He resisted the temptation to kick the door and withdrew into the waiting area with his tail between his legs.

In the meantime, the board meeting was progressing. Rolf was sitting at the head of the table, looking smart in his designer slacks, Churches loafers, a tailored open-neck shirt, and a blazer. Sabine looked fetching, with her hair in a French pleat, which showed up her excellent bone structure, a navy skirt, and a figure-hugging white blouse, as she reported the pleasing results their recent acquisition, Creative Electronics in Essex, a previous competitor, was continuing to produce.

Lord Britton, looking as suave and elegant as ever, had already confirmed the progress the two United States subsidiaries, Rolf Brenner Inc in Chicago and Dirk O'Reilly Inc in Atlanta, were continuing to make. Fenella Hardwick, the company lawyer based in New York, provided a brief update about Wall Street and related factors by video link. She also announced her plans to leave by the weekend for a break in the Rocky Mountains of Colorado.

Presentations by the plant's managing director and the directors of finance, public relations, and human resources also confirmed satisfactory progress all round. The young director of creativity and innovation, Penelope Jones, was the last item on the agenda for one of the most important aspects of the business, to present a fascinating focus on creativity and a tantalizing vision of the future. Her thought-provoking presentation generated much enthusiasm, including a round of applause for the brilliant young engineer.

Other business was generally predictable, but then Lord Britton passed a handwritten note to Sabine, who read the note, raised her eyebrows, nodded, and placed it in her briefcase.

As the team dispersed, Sabine said, "Rolf, quick chat with Nigel, just the three of us."

As they looked expectantly at Nigel, he smiled and then announced that off the record, several cells of subversive elements had become active in the British Isles and on mainland Europe.

Similar organizations had previously attempted to tarnish the reputation of Rolf Brenner Limited and its subsidiary in the United States, with the objective of generating doubts about the viability of the company and creating a dramatic fall in the value of the shares. Their ultimate goal had been to acquire the business at a knockdown price as part of their attempt which became known as the Spider's Web Incident.

As a result of Nigel's information, Rolf decided all security and intelligence activities would be reviewed and intensified, with immediate effect. In addition, he would renew contact with all senior law enforcement officers who had been involved with their company in the past.

These final discussions proved to be a constructive and positive conclusion to the proceedings, and the three of them relaxed and asked for more coffee, which Chloe duly served. Helen joined them to say a courier from the ministry of defence insisted on delivering a letter to Rolf in person.

"Ok, Helen, no problem," Rolf said, "wheel him in."

Chloe introduced the messenger, who glowered at the security guard who had been summoned by Helen to accompany him into the conference room and then to escort him to the exit of the compound. He was grumbling about having been kept waiting, waving a large sealed envelope around.

Nigel rose and approached the courier. "So you are Mr Harrison; thank you so much for your patience, and may I introduce Mr and Mrs Brenner, whom you wish to see."

"Yeah, mate, pain in the neck, making me wait; my boss will not be pleased."

"Just give him our compliments and say we are pleased with you and the efficient delivery of this envelope. Here's ten pounds for your troubles, and Richard will now escort you to your motorbike."

Albert grudgingly pocketed the bank note and for the second time this morning felt these Toffs had outmanoeuvred him. After his departure, the trio looked at the envelope, which was of an impressive plastic design to look like ribbed leather. The correct address was neatly printed on a framed label, and the total presentation exuded quality. There was also a smaller label marked with "Ministry of Defence."

"Right, let's see what we have been sent by Colonel McDavish-Brown," said Rolf, opening the envelope.

"Oh, no," Sabine whispered; Rolf looked thoughtful, Helen suppressed a scream, and Nigel's grim expression intensified as he extracted the contents from the envelope.

They consisted of a collection of high-quality paper with threatening, disturbing printed messages. Worse was to come when the second compartment of the envelope was opened, as it contained some horrific photographs and what looked like a North American Indian arrow.

Chapter 3

Narrow Escape: Northern Germany

Gerhard Albrecht was at the airport in Hamburg. He'd had a narrow escape from the authorities, made a snap decision, and went to the airport, where he bought a British Airways Club Europe ticket to Heathrow and then onwards, across the Atlantic, to report to the Master.

He had failed miserably in his mission, and he dreaded the wrath of Hannah Gerber, his section controller, and ever more so the mysterious owner of the organization, who appeared to be somewhere in the Rocky Mountains of the United States.

No one in the organization had ever seen him, except his section chief, but there were rumours about sinister deeds, unexplained disappearances, and natural disasters. Somehow, these appeared to be linked to a powerful organization that was denigrating and weakening a premium British company, Rolf Brenner Ltd, and their USA subsidiaries, RB Inc, as a prelude to a hostile takeover bid.

Life had been just perfect for Gerhard until twenty-four hours earlier, when things started to go badly wrong. And now, as he enjoyed his third bottle of the famous Flensburger Pilsner, he looked at the attractive label of the bottle and thought how ironic it was that all his carefully laid plans were shattered on the glacier, which was the source of the fresh water, that combined with the local Kristen barley was manufactured into this delicious beverage.

As the mellow, soothing effects of the beer gradually helped him to relax, he reclined in his comfortable armchair in the executive lounge and scrutinized the other passengers who were passing the time until their flight was called. A number of businessmen had removed their ties and were unwinding, after their three-day conference at the Messe, the giant convention and exhibition centre. Some ultra-smart ladies were still working on their laptops, talking on their mobiles, or leisurely leafing through the glossy magazines that were available, alongside a wide selection of English, German, and other national newspapers.

Gerhard got distracted by one of the attractive attendants, a tall statuesque girl who looked stunning in her uniform and assisted the club members with helpful attention and a dazzling smile. But more close to reality, who was that middle-aged male who himself seemed to be scrutinizing people and making notes? Maybe he had nothing to do with anything in the lounge, but all the same, it was essential to be alert to all those who might just be aware of the recent incidents near the glacier.

A young woman in a Jaeger business suit came into the lounge, looked around, and eventually settled in a chair; she crossed her long, shapely legs, picked up the *Tattler*, and started to leaf through the magazine. She looked irritated as the service attendant approached but then smiled and asked for a double espresso and a sparkling mineral water.

Gerhard felt confident he had made the right decision to come to this oasis of calm within the busy airport, away from the hubbub of the masses. Yes, the authorities were on the hunt for him because of his failure as a guide to lead a board of directors across the Flensburg glacier. But here in this lounge, he felt he was relatively safe, and it seemed unlikely those in power would look for him in this privileged environment. And why should anyone be looking for him, anyway? Hadn't he carefully eliminated any traces of his activities in the mountains behind Flensburg?

He was a highly skilled operator, having graduated from a petty criminal in the city centre of Hamburg, where he learned the art of survival in a tough environment, until he enlisted as a deckhand on an old fishing trawler of unknown origin and dubious ownership. Catching fish seemed to be a sideline, rather than a major part of the activities on board, and the young sailor soon learnt about the lucrative activities that allowed the crew and their captain to prosper.

Contraband goods, drug runs, and even human trafficking were all part of the plan until their luck ran out during a violent storm, with two men overboard and a giant wave that crippled the rudder, killed the engine, and ultimately left the trawler adrift, without power or steering. That's when the Coast Guard finally caught up with the target they had pursued for several months. Reinforcements soon arrived, boarded the trawler, and arrested the crew.

All of them except Gerhard, who was already far away, having unobtrusively jumped ship when their vessel met another trawler, a regular collaborator on the high seas. Olaf, the second in command of the Scandinavian vessel, hired him, and he became part of the crew.

His next move saw him returning to Germany, but this time, he avoided Hamburg, where he was known to the criminal community but also to the authorities who seemed to have observed his involvement with the fishing trawler for quite some time. This was the perfect moment for him to shave off his beard, groom his hair, switch from seaman's clothing to business attire, and start a flourishing business of import and export in nearby Flensburg.

A combination of his eighteen months on the trawler, observing and learning all the tricks of the shady trade, and his natural cunning allowed him to incorporate other elements within his business; one of these was to take on assignments of a criminal and violent nature. His right-hand man, Olaf, was experienced in arranging accidents and an expert in going in for the kill.

Gerhard, on the other hand, was clever and ensured that on the face of it, he remained a successful businessman and a pillar of the community. But those who needed a special task completed, including some subversive elements, knew whom to turn to if they wanted a dramatic solution to a problem.

One cold and blustery morning, with a storm brewing up from the Baltic Sea, Gerhard was approached and offered a major lucrative assignment, which would propel him into a senior position within a mysterious organization.

His instructions were provided in secret, without him ever meeting those who commissioned him to arrange a major accident to a group of industrialists who were on an excursion into the mountains to celebrate their successful board meeting.

After finalizing his plans in late afternoon, he was on his way to the bar where he regularly met with petty criminals, but also with major operators who controlled some of the syndicates that flourished in this neighbourhood. Suddenly, a roaring motorbike screeched to a halt alongside him; the rider dismounted, removed the helmet, and shook her shoulder-length, dark titian hair with a challenging smile.

"Come on, Mr Albrecht, time for a chat," the stunning woman said. "By the way, you may call me Boss. I am Hannah Gerber, your section chief, and the Master wants me to make sure you'll be ready to proceed in four days' time."

Gerhard, enthralled by the woman's commanding demeanour, said, "Wow, Hannah, what a pleasant surprise. Come on, let's have a drink and perhaps some fun?"

Hannah shot him a withering look and replied sharply, "Gert, boy, shut up, you little squirt. Here's what's going to happen: First of all, call me Boss. Never mention my name; second, at half past seven sharp, you'll proceed to the Eden Hotel, where I have reserved a discreet table in the Grill Room. There you will present your plans to me, and if I am not satisfied, I will crush your balls, understood?"

Gerhard nodded meekly and apologized; after the stunning apparition in black remounted her bike and sped off, disappearing around the corner, he went back to his base. Around seven, he slowly made his way to the hotel. The hostess led him to the reserved table and discreetly withdrew after offering coffee and mineral water.

Hannah had changed into a smart business suit for their meeting; she scrutinized every aspect of the plan of action and then cross-examined Gerhard; to his credit, she ultimately approved his plan.

"Just a warning, boy," Hannah said in her clipped voice. "Failure is not an option; it will not be tolerated, and you had better be aware, retribution from the Master is swift and without mercy. I've studied your background and modus operandi for several months and made him aware of your personal details, strengths, and weaknesses, and all your activities. Finally, believe you me, we will ruthlessly exploit them, just in case you do not succeed. Now, I bid you goodbye. I don't expect to hear from you until you confirm your first assignment was successfully completed."

Gerhard had been confident of success; he had followed the company that was being targeted, checked on the background and every detail of the five senior directors, spoke to the organizers of the journey into the mountains, and meticulously planned the timing and method of his attack.

Everything went wrong; the snowstorm hit the glacier where the five amateur mountaineers were traversing. An avalanche had been mined to thunder across the icy plain at a specific time, but it was triggered far too early and swept past the group; in a way, it cleared a path for them to return safely to their alpine hotel. The following day, they descended the mountain, returned to their homes, and celebrated the success of their organization.

A large contingent of police and mountain guides had moved in to handle the aftermath of the avalanche, and there was certain evidence that might have incriminated Gerhard's business. As a result, he wisely decided to escape and lay low for a while.

His worst moment came when he called Hannah Gerber to say he'd been thwarted in his attempt to eliminate the board of directors of the company. Her reaction was predictably devastating, commanding him to eliminate any trace of his connection with the organization and summoning him to Colorado by the weekend; he was to check in at the Denver Marriott Hotel and await further instructions.

He had been lucky to escape from the mountain but was able to do so because of his foresight, because of his ability to plan for every eventuality, and because he was an expert skier. Although he never contemplated failure, he had wisely prepared for an emergency exit, that saw him hurtling down the gorge through dense forest and miraculously disappearing from the scene.

So here he was now in the most pleasant, comfortable environment and delighted that any media coverage of the miraculous escape of five business executives from an avalanche on the Flensburg glacier was being maintained at low key. As he carefully leafed through the newspapers, he was heartened to see only a small paragraph in the broadsheets, little mention in the tabloids, and as he had seen and heard, only a brief reference on radio and television.

"Well done, Gert," he congratulated himself and in his mind ticked off his remarkable career: *Orphaned, bright but rebellious pupil at school, petty criminal in the harbour district of Hamburg, crew member on a fishing vessel with its main activity of a criminal nature, deserting the ship for a rival organization, transformation to a respectable business executive, leading criminal activities for those willing to pay, recruited by female section chief of a powerful new organization. First assignment unsuccessful because of weather, invited to meet the Master in Colorado. Bravo, Gert.*

These developments were just perfect as far as Gerhard was concerned and provided him with a substantial increase in confidence, as a result of which he called Olaf, his deputy, and instructed him to leak information that the chairman, Gerhard Albrecht, had embarked on a business trip to the United States and Olaf Hansson was now temporarily in charge.

In the meantime, several additional passengers arrived in the British Airways Executive Lounge; they were well looked after, served with refreshments, and settled down to await their departure.

The lady in the Jaeger suit looked up from her magazine and furrowed her brow, as an athletic, well-dressed man approached her seating area; he gave a slight bow and settled in an armchair opposite her, tapping away on his laptop and furtively glancing in her direction now and again.

Gerhard was relaxed as he observed the people in the lounge, but as he finished his refreshments, he grew uncomfortable and felt like he was under observation. He recoiled as a hand pressed down on his shoulder and a polished voice said in an English accent, "No need to jump, Albrecht, just look cool and don't worry. I am here to help, so here's a drop of Scotch, and I will explain."

The tall man standing over him looked impressive; he had a military bearing, accentuated by a perfectly trimmed beard and moustache. He wore an immaculate designer suit with suitable accessories, carried a Bally leather case, and gazed around the lounge with dark, penetrating eyes.

"My name is Colonel Tarrant, and here's the deal," the stranger said. "You cocked up big time, Albrecht, and I've been put in charge of your transfer to Colorado. By the time we reach the Rockies, I will have decided on what recommendations I shall discuss with Miss Gerber, our section chief, and what action we suggest to the Master. In the meantime, I will inform you of a major task tomorrow; by the time we reach Denver, you will develop a detailed plan and present it to me."

Although the colonel delivered these messages in a cultured and stylish way, Gerhard Albrecht felt intimidated by the complexity of this information. He was really looking forward to relaxing on his transatlantic flight, unwinding, enjoying excellent food and beverages, taking an afternoon nap, and then arriving in Denver to be met with new instructions. Instead, he was worried about the following day's journey, which would now be dominated by the presence of the colonel, and worse, he had to plan a major task.

These thoughts were interrupted when their flight was announced; Tarrant and Albrecht left the lounge, went to the gate, and boarded their flight. They arrived in London, spent the night at the Terminal 4 Hilton, and then resumed their journey to Colorado the following day.

Chapter 4

Betrayal: Switzerland

As dusk was gradually changing the views across the remote valley, Swiss Secret Service Sergeant Rita Liechti and Corporal Bruno Hintermann began to close down all the electronics in their underground observation post, lock up the post, and begin the precarious descent to their base.

Suddenly, they were alerted by noisy activities from across the valley, and the two operators consequently remained firmly glued to their instruments of observation.

Their attention was focused on the opposite side of the valley quite some distance away, to the right of the alpine farm, alongside the ascending slope. All had seemed peaceful a while ago, with no indication of disturbance, but now, there were loud noises, rumblings, shouted commands, and frantic activities.

Inside the mysterious building, tensions were high. Milton Adams's secret headquarters had been meticulously planned to include many special features not normally found in such an impressive construction, which looked like an oversized Swiss chalet. There were in fact rumours amongst the local farm hands of security guards arriving by helicopter, dragging prisoners into the vaults of the building. There was talk about dungeons and screams in the middle of the night.

Milton smirked as he surveyed the scenery below from his luxuriously fitted attic room; he had a spectacular view of the world below. There was no indication of any impending disruption to the peaceful surroundings of what seemed to be nothing more than a pleasant, domestic scene on a farm in the mountains.

He likened himself to a golden eagle soaring in the sky, using the thermals, looking for prey, and he had therefore named his sumptuous, panoramic room the Aerie. Yes, he had now sharpened his talons, would soar above all the others, identify his target, and then swoop down on his prey to take what was rightfully his. And no one, no individual, and no organization was going to stop him this time.

Two years earlier, his campaign had been so carefully planned, orchestrated in detail, and generously financed. That was until his executive team had miserably failed to deliver. Some of them had consequently paid the ultimate price, and in retrospect, he felt he had been too soft on the remainder of them, so further eliminations were quite possible. There would now be the beginning of a brutal and ruthless regime.

Milton was tall, athletic, and powerfully built; he looked distinguished, with a full head of grey, almost white hair and dark, jet black eyes, and a determined mouth, complimented by his rugged bronzed face. He wore a black sweater with army-style leather patches on the shoulders and elbows, adorned by a small golden spider emblem embroidered in front.

He liked to maintain a low profile, but he also enjoyed the company of women, especially those who gladly submitted to the special treatment he liked to administer. Such women somehow disappeared after their encounter with Milton Adams.

He had come a long way since his early days in the Hamptons, as the privileged only child of American parents. Their fatal boating accident off Long Island had shocked him but also left him as the owner of a huge fortune. Although a loner at school, he felt comfortable and happy to remain so.

After his graduation from Princeton with honours, he set himself up as manipulator of those in power with generous donations, achieving many of his objectives through secret and highly paid informants, and where needed, strong-arm tactics to further his goals.

Properties, organizations, and companies he acquired quadrupled the value of his empire, and had it not been for the failures of the imbeciles who let him down, his fortune would have grown further and blossomed with many more assets to his name.

Milton hated the memory of what he had failed to achieve because of the incompetence of individuals who were paid huge salaries to achieve their objectives; his temper rose as he recalled some of the details that had thwarted his plans. His fists crashed onto the antique desk in front of him, and he hit the cage holding his tarantulas, causing the deadly trio to scuttle into the sand at the base. He kicked Morgana's terrarium, and his beautiful snake hissed viciously, raising her head with her tail beating a loud and distinctive rattle.

After letting off steam, he relaxed and focused on the future, especially the dramatic developments that would happen later that day, providing he received the signal from his special informant to indicate the Swiss were planning to mount a full-scale attack. Well, he would show them who was really and truly in charge.

Milton glanced out the panoramic window and grinned as he thought what would happen; he walked across to his lavishly stocked cocktail cabinet. He reached for a Waterford brandy glass, poured himself a small measure of a vintage Cognac, took a sip, nodded, and topped it up.

He had always felt a great deal of pride in his Aerie, at the secret location of what he called the Web, which had been carefully constructed as a powerful and impregnable fortress, disguised as a large chalet of substantial proportions. It was situated in a valley that could only be reached through a secret labyrinth of caves. The occasional climber who found a way to the approach of the base and ventured closer had then mysteriously disappeared, never to be found and ultimately recorded as a victim of the dangers and unpredictability of mountaineering.

In the meantime, on the opposite side of the valley, life continued peacefully on the Alp. In Milton's personal environment, however, there was now considerable activity, and he summoned Musgrove, his chief of staff, for a final look at Operation Meltdown. He reviewed all the details of a plan that had been meticulously devised with military precision. He knew that hostile action from the Swiss authorities was now inevitable, and he was ready to thwart any attempt by them to close in on his empire.

Musgrove was a sinister individual who always wore a formal morning suit; he deferentially bowed as he entered the Aerie, carrying a steel executive case, chained to his wrist. He was short, almost dwarf-like, but muscular and powerfully built. His pale complexion was accentuated by jet-black hair, parted in the middle and slicked down on the side above ice-cold grey eyes, a bulbous nose, and a cruelly twisted mouth.

"Right, Musgrove," Milton growled, "you had better be ready with all systems in place for a perfect operation, once we hear from the mole."

"All problems sorted, sir, and ready to go."

"Problems? What problems? I do not tolerate this word, and bloody well get your act together, you ugly little toad."

"Sir, it's all systems go. I will explain the minor difficulty that I have completely resolved."

"Get on with it, then," Milton yelled, towering over Musgrove: "Check list, accountabilities, time schedule, evacuation, eliminations, big bang, and the finale."

"Sir, allow me to present you with the plan of action in chronological order, starting with the signal from our informer that will trigger my executive team to start the action by evacuating the farmer, his family, and their livestock through the woods, down the secret passage, and off the mountain, into the valley.

"This leaves you, sir, myself, Malik, our chief of security, and three guards, ready for takeoff at a moment's notice, in addition to Captain Schulz and his copilot, who have been put on red alert. The reserve pilot will fly the small helicopter, and I charged him with a special mission before he lands in northern Italy. Your secret files and personal possessions are packed and ready to go, and arrangements have been made for the transportation of the snake and the spiders."

At that moment, Milton's personal alarm sounded, interrupting the presentation. "Red alert, Musgrove," he snapped. "Top of the roof, stand clear of the door, and wait for the message; remember, no telecommunications at all, as the Swiss surveillance operators are ready to intercept and decode our messages."

Within a few minutes, Musgrove stepped out onto the roof of the building, stood aside of the service door, waited, and ducked as the whoosh of a crossbow bolt was followed by the sound of the wood, as the missile embedded itself into the centre panel of the door, where a black spot that indicated the target was pierced right in the middle.

The bolt was retrieved, carefully withdrawn, and presented to Milton, who decoded the encrypted message in seconds and then bellowed, "All systems go; jump to it, and no cock-ups, Musgrove."

"On my way, sir. All the charges have been placed, and Schulz has been ordered to cause havoc with the snow and the rocks on the ridge above our location as soon as we are airborne."

They heard the farmhands yodelling calls to encourage the herd of cows on the way, mingled with the barking of the dog who was pulling a cart with milk churns and wheels of cheese, as the farmer made a final roll call and locked the stables and Alp hut before joining the colourful cortege that soon disappeared between the trees.

"Rita, look, they are evacuating."

"Heavens, what's next? I know who's behind it, Bruno; someone engineered this exodus for all the occupants of the Alp to be safely out of the way, but what comes next? I just wonder."

At this moment, Bruno and Rita noticed the two black helicopters that had been prepared for takeoff were being attended to by engineers, and the flight deck crew seemed to be on high alert.

"Rita, look at the top of the building, behind the roof garden," called out Bruno. "Someone is moving towards the service structure; he's pulling at something in the door, and now he's running towards he stairs."

"I sense trouble, Bruno; you warn the boss while I watch to see what happens next."

"Yes, ma'am. I'll call the Colonel," Bruno said. "But look at all these people spilling out of the building; they all got aboard one of the helicopters, and now they started the engine."

The noise of the rotary blades intensified, and the larger helicopter took off, made a circle above the peaceful meadow, the Alp hut, and the chalet, and then hovered in front of the massive snow-covered peaks on the south-east side of the valley.

The smaller chopper was also in action, rising steeply and then hovering at the top of the snowfield above the building. Rita called Heiner, Peter Burki's chief of staff, but her conversation became inaudible because of a thunderous roar, followed by a series of explosions, which shattered the peace and quiet of the afternoon.

"Chaos here, Heiner; call back in a minute. We'll see what we can do."

Rita reached Bruno, who had left the observation post and was now standing opposite a scene of utter devastation, nothing, not the most rigorous training could have prepared the two young officers for the scenes of devastation they now witnessed. An enormous cloud of smoke rose above the giant chalet, which had been completely demolished and was still being rocked by secondary explosions as flames started to appear in between the debris.

But worse was to come, and although the larger chopper had disappeared beyond the snowy peaks to the southeast, the smaller machine continued to patrol the ridge above the chalet; the pilot fired four laser-guided missiles, releasing a massive avalanche and rock fall that thundered towards the Alp, engulfing what had been a meadow and an alpine farm and burying everything below the deadly mass of snow, ice, and rock.

And then an eerie calm descended on the scene of devastation in front of the two officers, with nothing left to do but to call HQ, report what they had witnessed during a relatively short period of about twenty minutes, and absorb the enormity of the devastation in front of their eyes.

Chapter 5

Danger: Switzerland

Corporal Hintermann and Sergeant Liechti took one last rueful look at the scene of utter devastation, heaps of smoking rubble, and the ruins of what had been a spectacular building.

"Just can't believe it, Bruno; as soon as we can establish contact, I want you to alert the colonel and his troops."

Round about the same time, Peter Burki was in full flow in front of the commanders of his elite troupe; they had been strengthened with members of Swiss Army grenadiers assigned from their unique training facility in Losone, a remote location in the wild mountain environment of the Ticino, the Italian-speaking canton of Switzerland.

"Your objective is to raid a mysterious chalet in a hidden valley in the central massive of the Swiss mountains," the colonel said. "There is a major threat within that building from a sinister new organization; we must stop them and snuff it out as a matter of priority.

"We now know the occupants are posing a major threat to a British company, and far more seriously, they are a real danger to individuals who may become victims of their ruthless actions, initiated by the leader, who is hiding in his secret building, which we are going to raid."

The colonel then pointed to the screen and said, "Our expert's ingenuity has provided us with perfect intelligence in consultation with our colleagues in the United Kingdom and the United States. Compliments to Commander Belinda Carrington, who finally cracked the code and located the source and future plans of this sinister organization."

The Molehill

Burki tapped on the board, which showed the location of their target. "Get ready for action. Tommy, you are in command. I leave it up to you to decide the exact time of the operation. Synchronize your watches, and evaluate the climatic conditions at 0300 tomorrow.

"This operation is important; do not hesitate to hit them hard. I have a feeling they may well anticipate the end is approaching. I therefore authorize you to use any weapons and force, and if need be, go in for the kill."

Just then, the door to the conference room flew open, and a member of the support team handed a message to the colonel, who looked at it briefly, frowned, and then boomed, "Alright, team, stand down; as I suspected, they knew our plans and bailed out, with an explosive and destructive end game."

Peter Burki was not easily disturbed, and his Bern bear character readily absorbed the news, filtered out any trivial details, and crystallized the elements that mattered.

He then said calmly, "You know I always mistrusted this devious, secret outfit, controlled by a ruthless individual who cunningly manipulates both his friends and foes. Our air force already confirmed the two helicopters' flight path, crossing the Alps near the Schreckhorn, in a south-easterly direction, on their way to the Italian Apennine Mountains and thereafter the hillside beyond. Our flight commander, Irma Bieri, in touch with the Italian Carabinieri and their air force, was ready to shoot down the escapees. I ordered them to follow them, see where they land, and throw a net of surveillance around their occupants, who will remain on our radar until we hunt them down.

"Tommy, order Sergeant Liechti and Corporal Hintermann to lock up their observation post and seal it. Thank them for their accurate observations and for coping with the unexpected disaster and turmoil. I now want them to descend from the mountain before nightfall. Strange that Armin and Sarah are still missing with no word or signal. Make sure to tell Bruno and Rita to look out for them on the way down, with orders for them to return to barracks."

Bruno and Rita took a last look at the devastation of what had been a peaceful alpine scene a few hours ago; they were determined to join the hunt for the villains. Having sealed the bunker, they carefully started their precarious way down the mountain, by climbing down through the dangerous crevasse.

"Bruno, for heaven's sake, secure your rope," Rita yelled. "Well done, Corporal; now throw the end loop to me."

"Careful, boss, crumbling rocks and a large precarious boulder above you."

"Phew, that was risky; now careful on the ice field, and watch out for the deep crevasses."

"Yes, ma'am, aaww baaalls," screamed Bruno, as he lost his footing and started a fast slide towards the cliff edge.

"Shut up, thicko," Rita snapped. "Look up, and grab this lasso." She accurately threw him the loop. "Now hold tight, carefully work your way to that sturdy tree stump, and secure the rope. Great, settle down; I'll be there in a minute; have you heard from Sarah and Armin?"

"Nothing, Sergeant, not a word; hopefully, we will find them enjoying a picnic on the meadow below, ha ha."

All attempts to reach their two colleagues by mobile or signals failed to produce any contact, which they diligently reported to base. As operations had been suspended, they were now able to make full use of their powerful searchlights to ease the final descent of their dangerous journey and guide them on their way.

As they reached the steep forest of pines, they relaxed and agreed that after their debrief by the colonel, they would enjoy a few drinks at the Roxy Club and then return to Rita's apartment for the night.

"Aw, good show," Bruno said with a cheeky smile as he complimented Rita on her perfect figure, accentuated by her tight jumper.

She giggled, grinned, and called him a naughty Bruni. And this is when their world was shattered, as they heard an agonizing cry that came from just below their position on the steep incline.

Rita glanced at Bruno.

"Jeessss."

He froze, listening. Then again the sound of someone in agony

"Corporal, handguns! You to the left, me to the right, pronto, and silent approach towards the precipice over there."

As they carefully descended, they heard another agonizing cry and followed the sound. Then Rita's light fell on Sarah's body, pinned to a tree and emitting another agonising sound.

"Aw, nooo," Rita said, reacting like lightning. "My move, Corporal; you cover me. There's danger all around us. Join me when the coast is clear."

As Rita reached Sarah, she saw an arrow had penetrated the right side of her chest; her eyes stared pleadingly. Her legs had buckled underneath her and twitched spasmodically.

"Bruno, that's a goddam arrow for f***'s sake; quick, help me to carefully pull it from the tree, and then we'll lay Sarah gently on her right side."

As they did so, Sarah's lips emitted several agonising sounds.

Bruno gave a vacant look and said, "It's a crossbow bolt, which are ..."

"Yes, yes, ok, Corporal, tell me later. Now call the colonel, order helicopter rescues, then search for Armin."

"The helicopter is on the way, Sarah, and you'll be fine," Rita said, gently stroking the young woman's hair, "but do you know where we might find Armin?"

Sarah shuddered and sobbed, "He tried to protect me, Rita, but was shot by a bolt through the neck, and then he fell down the cliff over there."

After a few minutes, two helicopters arrived; the first one lifted off and took Sarah to the nearest hospital, whilst the rescue services recovered Armin's remains from the base of the cliff.

Bruno and Rita were in the second helicopter, on the way to HQ for medical assessment and then reported to the colonel, who interrogated them for half an hour. He outlined their task of identifying the source of the crossbow and then told them to join the hunt for the assassin.

Chapter 6
War Council: Bologna, Italy

The last rays of the sun lit up the early evening on the foothills of the Apennine Mountains in the Emilia-Romagna region of northern Italy. There was no sound except for the melodious trill of a nightingale and the gentle tinkling of miniature bells, which were worn by the few goats that grazed not far away from the small monastery near the top of the hill.

The scenery was beautiful: forest-topped hillsides, the mighty mountains rising into the azure blue sky beyond, and further down, below the monastery, vineyards, ploughed fields, and a few houses, looking neat and colourful with their characteristic orange tiled roofs. In the far distance, the Reno and Savenna rivers glistened, and as the sun moved higher along the rocky cliffs beyond the valley, the solemn sound of the bells, calling the monks to vespers, could be heard.

Just then, the peaceful evening was interrupted by a distant mechanical clattering, not normally heard along this remote area of the country. After a while, it became clear that this was the noise of helicopters, preceding the appearance of two distant spots on the horizon, which gradually grew in size, became louder, eventually circled the slopes near the compound, and after a while gently settled down on the meadow.

Brother Anselmo had been alerted by signal about the planned arrival time of important guests; he was the only monk who knew about this visit. He was confident that he could count on the novices and, more importantly, his senior colleagues, who had learnt to obey and meticulously respond to his orders. They would therefore be ready to deliver the very special requirements of these eminent visitors.

Anselmo, the oldest son of an impoverished hillside farmer, had excelled at school, won a sponsorship, and did well at the theological college. Once ordained, he decided to enter the monastery as a novice, quite simply because he felt the many hours devoted to reflection would allow him to develop his ambitious plans for a future where he would be all powerful, manipulating others, achieving immense amounts of riches, and enjoying life to the full.

He rose swiftly through the ranks from his early days as a monk, and now he was the master of all the money, donations, income, and expenses. With cunning and guile, he became all powerful and free to operate in his own characteristic and ruthless style, whilst the frail and ageing abbot, Mario Machinello, was oblivious of all that was happening in his domain and quite content to remain in his cell for most of the time.

Anselmo was well known in northern Italy for his influence at the monastery, the way he used his power to achieve spectacular successes. People generally respected him but were also highly suspicious of the *Cormacchia*, the black crow, as they called him, because of his large beak of a nose, his piercing dark eyes, and the way he flapped his habit when confidently and flamboyantly strolled along.

Many of his transactions took place in the nearby town of Bologna, and one misty morning, as he was enjoying an espresso in the café overlooking the piazza, a young boy placed an envelope on the table in front of him and then ran away. There was just a short note inside, in ornate black calligraphy writing, saying simply "A business proposition will be presented to you, if you meet me near the chapel in the cemetery at noon today."

Anselmo was intrigued and yet suspicious, but he wanted to find out what this was all about. He decided to wait, hidden in the shadow of the chapel's portal, above the wonderful array of statues, ornamental creations, and elaborate headstones that adorned the graves. Shortly before noon, he noticed a powerfully built man in dungarees, a flat cap, and pale complexion; he approached a bench and took a seat.

Anselmo went over to the stranger from behind and then startled him by placing a heavy hand on his shoulder.

Once he recovered, the man greeted him, speaking in perfect Italian: "Brother Anselmo, my name is Musgrove, and you are a lucky man, as you have been selected from three thousand possible candidates to become a servant of one of the most powerful men in the world. We wish you to continue to carry out your functions at the monastery, but you would be entrusted with major developments that need to be undertaken on site, and most of all, you will be richly rewarded."

By midafternoon, Musgrove told Anselmo exactly what his task would entail and presented him with a down payment of several thousand euros in crisp new notes to fund the start of the structural changes that had to be arranged at the monastery. In addition, a substantial amount would be deposited into a Swiss bank account that was being arranged for his services.

Musgrove then explained, "Brother Anselmo, these changes need to be completed by early spring, in time for a visit by the Master and his senior team; you will be required to host the visitors for several days, providing lavish food, drinks, and most importantly, special entertainment for the all-powerful one."

During the next frenetic weeks of activity, Anselmo discovered the monastery had been built on the ruins of an ancient fortress, with dungeons and interconnecting caves which seemed to go on forever. He found an underground spring of mineral water, which was believed to contain healing powers.

"Mr Musgrove, sir, would you please come and have a look at an incredibly dramatic discovery?"

"What now, Brother Anselmo? Can't you see I am up to my neck in getting the exorbitant funds for this crazy project."

"*Si, Signore* Musgrove," Anselmo said and then thought, *Up to your squashed neck? You ugly, lazy idiot.* Then he stalked out of the office with his typical cormachio flapping of his habit.

Soon he heard footsteps and saw Musgrove running after him. "Brother Anselmo, sorry, may I now see your discovery please."

"*Certamente,* but be warned: It's dangerous and frightening. Follow me to the lower floor; there's a secret passage down a steep staircase."

At the bottom of the passage, the cool, air-conditioned environment was replaced by a roaring waterfall, which thundered passed small windows along the staircase.

Musgrove gasped as Anselmo led him deeper and deeper into the cavern at the foot of the steps.

"Fantastic," Musgrove exclaimed as he saw an enormous, calm underground lake, which took his breath away. "Brother Anselmo, you are a genius. This is completely soundproof, proving it's worth all the funds you have needed to finish the work and then send the crew back into the desert, where they are to disappear forever."

Later that day, Brother Anselmo was ready when the helicopters arrived; the visitors disembarked from the two helicopters. He greeted them and escorted them to their lavish suites that had been constructed in the caves below the monastery.

Shortly afterwards, the peace and quiet of the environment was once more interrupted, this time by the roar of a Harley-Davidson, which pulled up to the portal and was shut off; the rider, a shapely young woman, took off her helmet, shook free her Titian red hair, and demanded to see the Master.

"Welcome, Miss Gerber," Anselmo replied, adopting his typical humble monk's demeanour. "May I please show you to your suite? You may wait there until the bell rings in about an hour; I will then escort you to the dining hall, where your colleagues are due to gather."

Hannah simply nodded and followed the Crow into the caverns below the monastery.

"Ignorant cow," Anselmo snorted after leaving her in her suite. "But then genius Brother Cormachio has his own way of causing grief to arrogant Miss Nasty."

When it was time, Hannah entered the dining hall; Milton Adams stood at the sumptuously laden table and called out, "Glad to see you all made it on time, so here's a toast to the destruction of our target, Rolf Brenner and his factories and head office in England, plus his subsidiaries in the United States, resulting in my acquisition of his companies.

"All of you have shown your abilities in the past," he continued, "and this evening is a perfect moment for you to relax, enjoy an excellent meal and fine wine, and then return to your suite, where you will find detailed instructions about the tasks you are charged to accomplish. Tomorrow, I expect to hear from all of you about your impeccable contributions. My war council will be in session, and believe you me, I will tolerate no weaknesses, no failures; retribution will follow without mercy."

The following morning, a chorus of birds in the shrubbery and fields surrounding the monastery signalled the arrival of dawn. The regular tones of the bells added to the joyful noise. Milton Adams and several of the guests went on an early-morning hike along the path that bordered the forest above the compound, whilst others pursued physical exercises on the meadow below.

Breakfast was scheduled for eight o'clock, and the meeting started on time at nine thirty; Musgrove was dressed in his usual suit and flanked by two of his close assistants.

He bowed towards Milton, who was seated at the head of the large conference table, then turned to the other members of the council and said pompously, "Good morning, sir, ladies and gentlemen, I'd like to start by inviting you to thank Brother Anselmo for the enormous task in creating this superb facility for us."

This was followed by a round of applause.

"And now, Brother Anselmo," Musgrove continued, "would you kindly join your colleagues in the monastery? Please make sure the entrance to our domain is securely sealed. We'll let you know when your services are required later on this afternoon."

"Musgrove, stop waffling and get on with the business," Milton snapped. "I want to know the exact state of play of all your tasks to weaken Rolf Brenner Associates and all their subsidiaries. I want everyone associated with them to be scared, intimidated, and ready to capitulate.

"Any law enforcement agents on their side must be eliminated. I expect the shares of this microelectronics company to plummet, and then I will be seen as the noble saviour of this important company. One day, I'll tell you why this special company is absolutely essential for the next stage of my master plan.

"Musgrove, I want you to bloody well get on with it; tell me what the hell you are all doing, swanning about, spending my millions without presenting me with a return on my investment?"

Musgrove walked over to the electronic presentation board, flicked his handheld control, and brought up a map of Europe and Great Britain. "Please allow me to provide you with a summary of our successful activities in Switzerland, Germany, and England, before Miss Gerber adds further details of the operations that have been completed.

"I will start with yesterday's superb escape from Switzerland," Musgrove continued, "and the exemplary way we thwarted the Swiss Secret Service's intention to raid the Web."

"Stop your triumphant self-congratulations, Musgrove," Milton shouted, banging the table with his fist. "Had it not been through your incompetence, our secret hideout and my pride and joy would not have to be blown sky-high, so shut up, you ugly little dwarf, and get on with the business."

Musgrove frowned, looked peeved, but then grinned, as he was quite used to Milton's tirades, and then said, "Those who failed you, sir, will surely get their just desserts. In the meantime, I just hope you appreciate the brilliance of our underground facility here, which Brother Anselmo constructed according to my concept, design, and direction. And now with your permission, sir, we move on to Hannah Gerber's update about her section's recent activities."

Hannah was dressed in army camouflage and a black beret, her hair in a knot at the nape of her neck; she stood to attention, saluted Milton, and launched into a clipped, precise presentation delivered in perfect English but with a hint of a German accent.

"My contribution to defeat Colonel Burki's Swiss commandos was achieved by my mole, whom I trained to infiltrate the Swiss Secret Service. Further damage to their forces then followed, and I will provide you with details just as soon as they are available.

"So let us move on to Rolf Brenner Limited in UK," Hannah continued. "I had kept them under detailed surveillance for the past few weeks. My first move was to have a special package couriered from an untraceable source, handed over personally to RB, containing written and material items to deliver a stark warning of our intent for vengeance to the board of their company and particularly to Lord Britton, whom we well know through his role in the Spider's Web Incident.

"Ok, good progress, Gerber, carry on."

"Thank you, sir; this delivery is just an opening shot in a detailed campaign of threats and intimidation that will now gain momentum. If I may, I would now like to move to the plans for the United States, because the Brenners are shortly due to embark to southwest Florida, where they have an apartment on the barrier island.

"I therefore contacted Huntingdon and Petroni, who did well in Miami eighteen months ago, to increase the psychological pressure on the Brenners in a subtle and menacing way. I arranged for them to recruit a young artist and then to direct him to create drawings and paintings of such sinister subjects, that once delivered to Rolf and Sabine, and others who are in our way, they will start to generate fear and terror in the minds of the recipients."

"Finally, there is my German project, where I recruited a promising operator, who had already excelled in many areas covering the high seas and the city of Hamburg, and now, as a successful criminal, disguised as a respectable, law-abiding businessman. His task was to enable our acquisition of a major German electronics company, and when he messed up, I was tempted to kill him off but decided to put the cunning little bastard under Tarrant's ruthless control for the Colorado project.

"And just to conclude, I have my team keeping a close watch on Manhattan's prestigious Central Park South and particularly Fenella Hardwick, the Brenners' celebrated lawyer, who was such a thorn in our eyes eighteen months ago. She is due to go on an outbound holiday in Colorado in a few days, and I have prepared some nasty surprises for her in the mountain wilderness that will deliver a clear message of our intent."

"Ok, Gerber," Milton interrupted. "That's a clear and precise summary of what's been done; good. But you had better fill in the many gaps I have already identified; Musgrove and I will now cross-examine you about exactly what we have achieved, because I can't see it, except plenty of very clever words. Come on, girl, what the hell is actually going to happen now?"

Hannah smiled and began to answer, but just at that moment, Milton's phone signalled an alert. He scowled, checked the message, and bellowed, "Musgrove, immediate helicopter scramble; war council resumes tomorrow at 0830 sharp. Now all of you bloody well get your act together, and if you don't have all the details of what actually happened and a precise battle plan, there will be all hell to pay."

Chapter 7

London: Heathrow T4

Commander Belinda Carrington of the British Secret Service gave her military escort some final instructions, and then she strolled into Terminal 4 at London's Heathrow Airport.

The departure concourse was crowded and lively on this Wednesday afternoon. Passengers were milling around in their thousands, representing the colourful kaleidoscope of a truly international, gregarious, and multicultural population. As some of them gathered in the comfortable seating areas near the wide panoramic windows they could see the gigantic array of cranes towards the west of the airport, where Terminal 5 was being constructed, to be opened in a few years' time.

The concourse was buzzing with prestigious retail outlets featuring premium brands, doing a roaring trade only equalled by their neighbouring stores where utilitarian and popular goods contributed to the remarkable amount of turnover that was recorded at Heathrow every day.

Restaurants and all sorts of hospitality outlets were doing excellent business; they offered a variety of food and beverages, in a way that was specifically tailored to the needs of busy passengers who demanded quality, choices, speed, and good value for money. There was a wide selection of outlets, ranging from the most popular to the more exclusive.

The fast-track security check area, reserved for first class and business class passengers, was busy, but an efficient team of friendly staff kept waiting times to a minimum, and passengers soon collected their belongings just beyond the control gate.

Belinda Carrington approved of tight security measures, and as part of her legendary expertise in fighting international and organized crime, she was intensely aware of the dangers posed by some of the world's fanatical elements and the newly emerging crime barons who had infiltrated commerce.

Today, she was on a different mission, however. Her normal occupation was a senior agent for MI6, the UK's Secret Service, with their head office and central operations situated alongside the River Thames, not far from London's Parliament Square.

On this occasion, she was finally leaving London for a well-deserved break and ten days of creating her own space, to reflect and hopefully come to terms with the tragic events just six weeks to the day that had dramatically changed her life, when Colonel MacTavish of the Scots Guards called her and gently broke the news that Belinda's fiancé, Major Duncan Stewart, had been killed by a sniper in Kosovar.

Now subsequent to all the necessary formalities, culminating in a memorable funeral, military honours, and a special award, she needed to find peace and contentment in the solitude of the high prairies and mountains of Colorado; she also planned, in her typical style, to celebrate Duncan's memory in her own very special way.

Belinda's destination today was Denver, where she would hire a powerful four-wheel drive vehicle and head off to Boulder in order to establish an initial base and meet up with Professor Duncan Cameron, whose daughter Fiona had faced mortal danger on her assignment in Florida eighteen months ago.

Duncan Cameron was lecturing at the University of Colorado and had invited Belinda to present her expert approach of fighting the dark elements that now threatened to infiltrate peaceful towns throughout much of the Western world. Her successful contributions to eliminate subversive organisations were well known, and the professor's students were full of excitement in anticipation of meeting their heroine, who had already established herself as one of the most accomplished crimefighters of her time.

After a few days in Boulder, she would then head to the famous Flatiron Mountains for the first stage of her outbound adventures, prior to going further into the majestic Rocky Mountains, where she intended to find peace, come to terms with the past, and establish the basis for a dynamic, fulfilling, and exciting future.

After collecting her hand luggage and burgundy coat, she leisurely wandered along the retail stores and enjoyed a spot of window shopping; she contemplated some purchases but finally decided to relax at the seafood bar, which is situated towards the eastern end of the concourse. A delicious plate of lobster and smoked salmon, enhanced by a glass of champagne, further increased her feeling of wellbeing.

Francois, the manager of the bar, immediately recognized Belinda but used his professional discretion in addressing her simply as "Madam." There was no indication he knew who this striking young lady was, nor that his own role as one of her informants was anything else than that of a courteous restaurant manager.

The other patrons of the seafood bar this afternoon consisted of some retail managers on their way to a conference in the Far East, two couples in their early sixties travelling to Florida in order to board their cruise liner at Fort Lauderdale the following day, and a young couple who were clearly at the start of their honeymoon.

Nothing unusual, until Belinda found a brief note discreetly tucked into her receipt she settled just a few moments ago. Three particular individuals had been spotted that morning; two of them arrived from Chicago and the other one came from New York. Two known criminals had left the airport for a destination in the Caribbean.

By the same token, there was a strong indication that three shady characters were currently in transit, having arrived from Marseilles at Terminal 1 just after eleven a.m. and then transferred to intercontinental departures, with their destinations yet to be determined.

Airport security in the special police force responsible for this volatile area had been informed and were on the case, which Belinda noted with considerable satisfaction and a true sense of relief that any possible complications were in safe hands; she was now able to leave the UK with a clear conscience and reassured about Heathrow's level of security.

The Molehill

She decided to walk to the other end of the concourse, just beyond Gate 1a, where she was later to embark, and enjoy the luxury of the Executive lounge, which BA had launched just a few weeks earlier. As she purposefully strode along the shopping mall, she was aware of admiring glances that followed her progress along the row of premium retail outlets.

"Well, so I am turning heads now", she thought with a mischievous smile, as she spotted her image in the mirrors of a display. And yes, she looked striking in her smart outfit she had chosen for her journey: a bronze silk blouse with breast pockets, Cossack-style trousers, calf-length leather boots, a loose safari style jacket, and her burgundy Burberry coat.

She checked into the lounge, which was pleasant and relaxing, particularly the quiet area upstairs, immediately beyond the lively chef's theatre, where meals were prepared to order and not far from the tempting wine-tasting area. An interesting mixture of passengers enlivened the lounge, and Belinda studied them on the basis of her professional expertise but also out of her natural curiosity.

Most of them looked quite pleasant, consisting of the normal mix of international business executives, a group of medical consultants (based on their jargon and comments). There were also a few elderly leisure travellers who clearly enjoyed the privileges of Premium Class travel.

Belinda was sure she recognized a young man in jeans, t-shirt, and trainers sporting several tattoos and earrings in the shape of a guitar, wearing headphones and engrossed in a tune that sent his feet tapping, as a rising celebrity on the country pop circuit. This is when she first heard the unmistakable sound of the southern French accent, so distinctive and characteristically spoken in the delta of the river Rhone.

The senior gentleman of the group was sounding off about *"les Ros beef,"* as the French sometimes like to call English people, and how expensive British Airways was, and "oui," they had served him an excellent breakfast, but otherwise, they were not nearly as good as Air France.

He had a red face with a large nose, thick lips, and a perpetually superior look on his face; he took a deep breath, looked challengingly at his colleagues, took a gulp of his cognac, and continued with this tirade by almost shouting that in any case, the French airline did not even have a direct flight to London today when he wanted one, and he did not wish to change airplanes in Paris, and in any case, Air France did not fly to Denver.

His two travel companions raised their eyebrows but acknowledged the well-dressed man, who wore an elegant, lightweight cream suit with a crimson red open-neck shirt; he appeared to be the leader of the group.

"Come on, Luc, am I not right about this stupid French airline?" he demanded and. "And Hubert, don't slurp so much of this red wine, which I have to say BA chose well, to my surprise, because the English don't know anything about food and wine, not like us, the masters of culinary excellence."

Belinda suppressed a smile at this passionate outburst and continued to study the trio and their conversation, which seemed to turn into an argument, with arm and hand movements accompanying an ever-more-heated exchange, until the man called Hubert stormed off and defiantly refilled his glass, after tasting several wines which were displayed for travellers to sample and enjoy.

Hubert wore jeans, leather boots, and a mustard yellow Provencal-style shirt with a squiggly red and black motif, similar to the attire worn by the Gardiens, the bull herders who rode the white Camarque horses, carrying the traditional trident to prod the beasts. Belinda studied his craggy, leathery, and weather-beaten face and noted his short but impressive physique.

The third individual, Luc had sharp, pointed features and small dark eyes, which perpetually darted all over the people in the lounge. He had a pale complexion, gelled black hair, a thin moustache, and a perpetually inquisitive facial expression. He also wore Provencal-style clothing but of a more stylish nature than Hubert, consisting of a light blue shirt with black motifs and a black string tie, complemented by light trousers and a black velvet jacket.

As the three of them reconvened, Belinda overheard the plans they had after arrival in Denver; she was surprised about their naivety in loudly conversing in their French language, clearly under the impression no one else in England would be able to comprehend their exchanges, let alone the details of their debate. As their conversation became ever more

The Molehill

animated, they were unaware how intently the beautiful young woman nearby listened to them.

The animated trio failed to notice the young lady was now taking copious notes in her small Smythson's notebook, and as she did so, her mind wandered back to a transatlantic flights from just over eighteen months ago. On that occasion, she had tailed a suspect between Zurich and Miami, and the resultant events developed into a dramatic, dangerous sequence: being kidnapped, eventually fighting her way to freedom, and then defeating the criminal elements involved.

Now on this journey, she hoped for relaxation and for adventure of a different kind, of physical challenges, outward-bound activities, and plenty of opportunity to breathe fresh air under the stars. But at the same time, she decided to keep a close watch on the trio, whose careless descriptions about a nasty boss woman and plans for Colorado made them a target for investigation. Some of the details were now documented in Belinda's notebook and engrained in her mind, just in case.

her flight was finally called, and as she walked ahead of the three Frenchmen, she continued to overhear further snippets of their conversation.

The Welcome at the gate was friendly, and a cheerful steward took great delight escorting Belinda to her business class aisle seat; he offered to take her jacket, which she declined, but readily accepted a glass of champagne, Macadamia nuts, and a copy of the *Daily Telegraph*.

As she relaxed in her comfortable seat, she noticed two further arrivals sitting just to the left, in front of her. One of them was a tall, bearded man, being addressed by the steward as "Colonel Tarrant.." His travelling companion looked impressive in a different way: muscular, with a good head of light brown hair, strong bushy eyebrows, and a weather-beaten face.

Something about the military man triggered memories in Belinda's razor-sharp mind; she was not sure whether it was his upper-class accent or the way he walked or his general movements. In any case, Belinda added Colonel Tarrant to her list of people under observation, and she was quite confident she would discover some hidden depth and whatever might have happened in the past.

Colonel Tarrant, or whoever you are, I will keep my eye on you during the flight, Belinda thought. *I will set my US agent on your trail, once we land in Denver.*

the captain introduced himself over the intercom, mentioned the members of cabin crew of the 767, and reminded passengers to pay attention to the safety briefing; shortly after, chocks were off, the aircraft taxied onto the runway, and waited for clearance, ready to take off to the Rocky Mountains in Denver, Colorado, where dramatic events and unexpected dangers awaited.

Chapter 8

Investigations: Switzerland

Colonel Peter Burki had been in his top-floor office since five o'clock, reflecting on the events that had so dramatically changed the investigation into the mysterious organization. Peter had concluded an informant had tipped off the head of the sinister organization about the precise time of the elite troupe's attack.

His team had located the secret valley in the Alps and were just about to mount a full-scale attack. The messenger arrived during Peter's final briefing and announced news about the dramatic developments that had occurred seventy-eight miles away to the east of the barracks, where they were all assembled.

Peter had received the news in his usual calm and decisive way, booming out orders, withdrawing his troops from their observation post, and launch an investigation about who had tipped off the subversive organization. His instructions were clear, and he assured everyone that those responsible would be hunted down wherever they might be and eliminated.

He had issued orders to Sergeant Rita Liechti and Corporal Bruno Hintermann, who arrived at Wankdorf, the national football stadium, ready to join his senior agent, who was briefed about his mission to identify the active crossbow traitor.

Peter Burki was now standing at the large gothic window that faced the old town of Bern, surrounded by the river Aare, with a splendid view of the hills and snowy mountains beyond. He took another puff of his pipe and then finished his coffee, picked up his notebook, and went down the stairs, past the security guard, and outside the old office block.

As he walked down towards the mighty bridge and the lower parts of the town, he was pleased about the good news from University Hospital. Sarah, his young operator, had been shot through the chest with a crossbow bolt, but was now well on the way to recovery. This unknown assassin was also responsible for killing Armin, one of Peter's most promising young agents, who had shielded Sarah but was tragically struck in the neck by a crossbow bolt and plunged two hundred meters into the canyon below.

Peter now strode along with great purpose, descended the hundred and twenty steps down to the river, and then marched along the quay until he reached another smaller bridge with a number of workshops, shacks, and a few desolate warehouses.

Towards the back of the development, he walked through a maze of scaffolding and other building materials until he rounded a corner and smelled the giveaway aroma of Amsterdam tobacco. Sure enough, his old friend, fellow professor, and confidant was peacefully sitting on a makeshift bench, quietly puffing away at his pipe, looking at Peter with steel blue eyes above his pince-nez with a conspiratorial smile. He was dressed in traditional farmer's clothes, a blue smock and black trousers, and he wore a jaunty hat with an eagle's feather on his mop of snow-white hair. He carried a shepherd's crook, and a Bernese mountain dog sat calmly in front of him, but with alert eyes scrutinizing the visitor.

"Good morning, Tobias, you look ready for action."

Peter smiled as they shook hands.

"Thanks for coming at such short notice, and hello there, Barry," as he made a fuss of the dog, who immediately responded by wagging his tail. "Well now, Peter, I already know what's in the public domain about the self-destruction of the mysterious organization in the centre of the Alps. And of course I have also found out some peculiar angles that may lead us to the source of the betrayal."

"Let me fill you in about the latest details, in addition to the results of my personal investigations; it's shaping into a jig-saw puzzle, Tobias."

The two friends spent nearly two hours, discussing the situation, and

The Molehill

then walked along the river Aare until they reached an old restaurant, where they enjoyed some refreshments before parting for their very different ways.

Peter returned to his office before being flown by helicopter back to the secret valley, where forensics were busy combing the debris from the incident. At the same time, Tobias made his way further along the river and started a pilgrimage he knew would lead him to the traitor who alerted the sinister organization about the impending raid on their secret base. Moreover, he would also pursue identifying the assassin who had fired the lethal crossbow missiles.

About sixty kilometres to the north-west of Bern, the peace of the meadow was interrupted by the large and powerful tractor, which roared along the crest of the field and eventually chugged to a halt near the big barn. Ueli Amberg was pleased with the morning's work of tending his parents' farm.

He had mended the fence and secured the gate that kept their eighty Simmental cows safely on the field to the west of the estate. Ueli fetched a strong coffee and a bottle of water from the kitchen and then ambled into the barn, followed by Nero, his black Labrador, and the two border collies, Max and Moritz. He found a convenient seat on a bale of hay because he needed time to do some serious thinking; Maya, his girlfriend, had once again disappeared.

He tried her handy, but it went to voicemail. Maya was not in the small apartment the two of them shared in Fislisbach, a village near the small town of Baden, not far from Zurich and the international airport.

Ueli then called the stylish and fashionable store where Maya worked, but her manager said she was away on leave. Next, Ueli contacted the concierge at the apartment building where Maya was housekeeping for her cousin Pia, a flight attendant. No, said Mr Muntwiler, Miss von Gunten had not been seen for several days.

What worried Ueli was that Maya's mysterious absences were becoming more frequent. Each time this had happened up to now, Maya always provide him with a plausible explanation. She had been to visit her grandmother in the Kanton of Valais or a cousin in Locarno, and yes, she had to travel to Solothurn to arrange her forthcoming class reunion.

He was really disturbed by the changes to her personality, which was normally sunny, happy, and ebullient. Lately, however, she became pensive and sat quietly, brooding and sullen, snapping at Ueli when he tried to lift her spirits and simply being objectionable. This usually happened just before she disappeared and then stayed away for anything between two and ten days.

When Maya eventually returned, Ueli was always overjoyed, but these times also worried him, because of her hyperactive moods. Yes, she was happy and loving towards him; she oozed with sex appeal and was wildly ravenous when she demanded that he make love to her. She often brought him presents, and then again her demeanour was inevitably overexuberant, hyper, and at times quite frightening.

Ueli happened to be a steady, confident, capable, diligent, and successful young farmer who managed his parents' estate with energy and determination, making substantial progress in moving the business forward.

With his two feet firmly on the ground, he was strong and dependable, but he completely failed to understand the subtleties of the female mind. At the same time, he resolved to identify the cause of Maya's mood swings and he was determined to help her to adjust and make her happy.

Meanwhile, not far away from Fislisbach, there was a modern building in the old part of the small town of Baden overlooking the river; it was beautifully appointed, housing a lavish reception area on the ground floor, thriving businesses on the first and second floor, and luxurious apartments of various sizes above. Pia Marinello, a senior flight attendant, lived on the fourth floor but was often away due to her busy schedule, which regularly took her away to the United States, the Far East, or South Africa.

Pia loved the excitement and privilege of working for one of the world's premium airlines; she enjoyed interacting with so many different people and developed her studies for what she was confident would develop into an exciting and rewarding future. At twenty-seven years old, with a degree in economics and international commerce, she was glad she had abandoned the boredom of her first job as a junior manager in a stuffy merchant bank in Zurich.

The Molehill

Two boyfriends had come and gone, with her blessing; they had not left any gaps in her life because her world was full of excitement, pleasure, enjoyment, and hard work, but it was totally suited to her gregarious and engaging personality. She loved returning to her calm and relaxed lifestyle in between duty travels and enjoyed her leisure time, seeing friends and family, and pursuing her studies.

Pia's cousin, Maya von Gunten, kept her apartment in perfect order during her frequent periods abroad, cleaning, attending to the laundry, sorting Pia's mail, and stocking her refrigerator prior to the young woman's return to Switzerland. She loved entering the stylish reception hall, teasing Anton, the porter, taking the elevator to the fourth floor, and entering the beautifully appointed rooms, relaxing and pretending they were hers.

On this particular day, Anton was in his element because his boss, the concierge, Mr Muntwiler, was away and had placed him in charge. Besides running the shop, Anton was a source of general information about the companies operating in the building and about the residents.

He was always cagey with the treasure of his knowledge, but once he identified those who mighty reward him with Swiss francs, he could be persuaded to pass on some secrets. Anton was short in stature and looked like a benevolent monk, with his round face, staring blue eyes behind round steel-rimmed glasses, a potbelly, and a green porter's apron that circled his considerable waist.

Anton rubbed his hands at the thought of the cash he had accumulated and the additional deals he might be able to complete on this particular day. And then he noticed Miss Marinello's elegant housekeeper, who stood in the entrance of the building.

"Miss von Gunten, you look decidedly glamorous," Anton enthused. "And what a striking outfit you are wearing today."

"Come on, Anton, don't go mad now; it's not so special, just my normal way of elegance and style," teased Maya, as she proceeded to the elevator and disappeared with a dismissive wave at the old man, muttering, "Silly old fool."

Anton, in the meantime, had become quite thoughtful; he paced the floor of the reception area, frowning and mumbling to himself, trying to get to the bottom of what was bothering him about Miss von Gunten. It was not her flippant remarks she invariably aimed at him, nor her mischievous sense of humour, but many years of watching and observing people had taught him to notice unusual details in behaviour.

Maya had soon completed some minor duties: opened the windows, checked and sorted Pia's mail, and thoroughly cleaned the apartment. But then she decided to treat herself to me-time, stripping off and luxuriating in a fragrant warm bath, with plenty of exciting thoughts on her mind. Yes, soon it would be time for her next move and another step towards the untold wealth she planned to secure for her future.

She had always envied her cousin's lifestyle, her regular travels to faraway places, the luxurious purchases she brought home, and the carefree happiness the young flight attendant enjoyed. This was exactly what Maya wanted to achieve, and the day to launch her dramatic plan was not far away. As she relaxed in her bath, she thought about her boyfriend, strong, powerful Ueli; she wanted him to make love to her, which increased her sensuous feeling, and as her mind wandered from her boyfriend to the new and mysterious contact in her life, her feelings intensified and became more sensuous, culminating in the ultimate sensation, which engulfed her in a crescendo of pleasure.

Chapter 9

The Studio: Queens, New York

Valentino Cuccione poured himself another glass of Chianti Ruffino from the bulbous, wicker-encased bottle his mother had presented to him on the quay at Genoa, just before he boarded the mighty ocean liner to the New World.

He well remembered the emotional farewell at the quayside, where several dozen members of his extended family had gathered to wish him farewell. After a while, the moment come to say good bye, and Valentino board the wonderful ship with its mighty funnels.

As the majestic liner left the moorings, progressively gaining speed, Valentino stood, waving at the railings, and for quite a while, he heard the wailing cry of "Valentino, Valentino, Valentino," drifting across the water, as the shoreline gradually faded away. He then returned to his shared quarters and prepared to start his first shift as a waiter, later that day.

This now seemed a long time ago, and here he was, three years after his arrival in New York and living in a small but neat apartment in Queens; on this day, he was celebrating the fantastic news he had received. He simply could not believe his good fortune and the way his life would now dramatically change, forever.

He wished Orsina, his girlfriend, was here to celebrate, but she was in Maine, competing with her college team. So he poured himself some more wine and enjoyed a plate of Italian salami and some slices of Parmesan cheese. After his fourth glass of Chianti, he turned his CD player all the way up and raised his voice in unison with the singer, who melodiously intonated *"Come Prima, Come Prima, Tie Amero,"* with Valentino bellowing at the top of his voice.

After a while, his singing grew worse but also louder, until the neighbours started to knock on his wall, telling him to shut up and be quiet in no uncertain terms. Valentino rushed into the corridor and knocked on all the apartment doors, shouting in his Italian accent, "Sorry, sorry but I am inviting you all to join me for a celebration party, so welcome, my friends, and enjoy."

His invitation was met with true cosmopolitan enthusiasm, contributions from the other tenants, some from the Far East, from Germany, and from Eastern Europe, and as a result, the party developed into an international festival of food and drink that went on until the early hours of the morning.

Just after midnight, the festivities were interrupted by the ringing of the telephone, which Valentino eventually answered, then held the receiver away from his ear in order to reduce the decibels of the onslaught in Italian his girlfriend unleashed, because he had failed to call her earlier that evening., as promised. He listened patiently, with an embarrassed grin on his face, and eventually managed to pacify her by promising to give her some wonderful news when she returned to New York on the weekend.

The next time the telephone rang, it was seven thirty in the morning, about three hours after Valentino had eventually said, *"Buona notte"* to his neighbours and collapsed on his bed. As he sleepily answered, "Hello, good morning," the loud voice at the other end made him jump out of bed, to listen; he listened to the terse message that was delivered to him in a cultured American accent: "Mr Cuccione, your instructions will be handed over to you at a secret place, with time and date to be advised."

"Yes, sir, sorry, madam, and when will I hear?" Valentino managed to say, but the caller had rung off.

Valentino felt slightly uneasy about this development and thought about it for a moment, but then he decided to take a refreshing shower, revive his metabolism with several cups of strong espresso, and recharge his batteries with a large slice of Panettone, some cheese, a couple of pears, and a few grapes.

The Molehill

Next, he called Orsina, who was surprised but delighted to hear from him, just as she was leaving for a fitness training session. She giggled when he told her about his mad singing the previous evening, explaining why he forgot to call and his vivid description of his neighbours and some of their antics. Most of all, she was intrigued about the fantastic news he promised to present to her when he met her at Grand Central Station.

Valentino was due on an afternoon shift later that day and had ample time to tidy his apartment from the previous evening's festivities; he brewed an espresso and then relaxed in his armchair to reflect on his adventures after coming to New York three years ago.

He had found a small bedsit room in Queens; the rent was not too high, which allowed him to send monthly funds to his family in Bologna. His job as a waiter not far away from his lodgings had initially been modestly paid minimum wage, of course. But this was just the beginning of his time in the United States and he always vowed this would not remain so for long, because he would progress, become successful, and earn good money as time went on.

His Mediterranean charm and vitality soon proved to be a valuable asset, which pleased his manager at the diner and was appreciated by the customers, many of whom asked to be served by the young man from Italy. The tips he earned were substantial, and in due course he was promoted to a more senior position, and his fortunes started to gradually improve.

As things progressed, he become a popular member of the local Italian community, and then he met Orsina, a voluptuous Mediterranean beauty who captivated him with her flamboyant personality and an engaging smile. Her jet-black hair hung in ringlets, framing a classical face with a perfectly shaped Roman nose, above a sensuous mouth, and lit up by large dark eyes that sparkled under thick eyebrows.

Back in Italy, one of Valentino's greatest pleasures was creating paintings and drawings that delighted his tutors; they provided him with excellent grades at college and a bright future. He seemed destined to develop his future at a famous academy of arts, until the money ran out and he embarked on his journey to the United States.

All this had happened in the distant past, of course, and as his income continued to improve, he decided to enrol at the local school of arts, where he became an enthusiastic pupil; after a couple of years, he graduated and contemplated whether he could make a living from creating drawings and the occasional oil painting. Having considered all probabilities, however, he wisely decided to focus on his career in the hospitality business and pursue his artistic ambitions in his spare time, as a hobby.

Painting and drawing therefore remained a side line, but in due course, Valentino entered a few competitions and was successful He was invited to exhibit some of his work at the local festival of arts and in the community library. It was a modest start, but a local newspaper printed an upbeat critique about this young up-and-coming artist.

Valentino took great delight drawing and painting Orsina at every opportunity, not just on her own but occasionally with her teammates, training and competing against other colleges. He also brought to life some of the more memorable events that he observed, from simple encounters to dramatic demonstrations, styled to depict all the joy, the passion, and the pleasure of life.

Critics liked his unique style and praised the vitality and drama of his paintings, especially how he accurately illustrated some recent events that captured the imagination of the general public. Local radio also showed an increasing amount of interest, with the occasional interview on air and an invitation for him to be a guest at a phone-in programme.

The growing interest in his works and being quite well known locally were gratifying, but sales of his paintings and drawings remained modest until his exhibition at the local library, when a strange encounter alerted him that someone, somewhere was taking an interest in him or in Orsina perhaps or even his work.

One Saturday afternoon during a successful exhibition at the library, the two of them noticed a distinguished man in a dark suit and an attractive blonde woman observing those entering the exhibition from across the road. They were sitting at a bistro table, outside the cafe opposite the library, but kept on glancing in the direction of the entrance and at one stage seemed to use a pair of binoculars, looking at some starlings on the roof, but then visibly lowering the glasses to focus on the exhibition. Then suddenly, they disappeared into thin air.

Slightly disconcerting as this was, it also intrigued the young couple, particularly when another encounter, in the park, further confirmed there were some mysterious individuals about. One glorious, sunny morning, the two of them were strolling past the sports stadium and then through the wooded area that flanked the wide expanse of well-kept lawn.

They had just crossed the picturesque bridge across the stream and were walking down the path towards the playing fields, when they spotted a metallic glint in the shrubbery, close by, followed by several clicks that sounded like the shutters of a camera.

Valentino immediately went to investigate but was only able to hear footsteps and breaking twigs in the undergrowth ahead. At the same time, Orsina had approached the small wooded area from a different angle; she called for Valentino, when she suddenly heard a sound behind her and felt a push to the middle of her back that sent her sprawling into the bushes. She saw a shadow disappearing around the corner, shortly followed by the sound of a heavy motorbike that gradually faded away.

Orsina, annoyed about the indignity of her stumble, brushed herself down and exclaimed, *"Mama mia, porco maiale,"* as Valentino rushed around the edge of the woodland, looking worried but laughing at her expletives. The young girl reassured him that she was fine, and holding hands, they then made their way to Orsina's home, treating the episode in the woodland with their customary sense of humour, by mimicking the mysterious person in the bushes and then on the motorbike with funny voices and by bursting into fits of laughter.

Finally, Friday night after their successful exhibition, Tim Warner, their journalist friend, received a mysterious telephone call and reported it to them.

A lady called who spoke in a cultured accent with a Southern twang; she said, "Hi, Tim, we recently met at a press reception, and I was so impressed by your column in the local media. Now I am researching new and promising artists for a major publication, and following your article about Valentino Cuccione, I need some more information about this young up-and-coming Italian."

"Well, thanks for your nice feedback, but tell me, who are you? And who are you working for?"

"Tim, I thought you would remember me, Daphne, strawberry blonde with ponytail, and we had such fun when we met."

"Sorry, Daph, can't remember, and you know any information I am able to pass on to you will already be in the public domain. By the way, what's your surname and details about your employer?"

"I'm Daphne Jones, and my assignment is secret, so I can't give you those details."

"Well, Miss Jones, this is the point where our conversation ends; good luck with your project." Tim frowned as he terminated the call; he looked for a caller ID, but as he expected, it had been withheld. *Strange approach*, he thought; *I better report this to good old Vallo.*

Valentino, who prided himself on his knowledge of English literature, said, "Thanks, Tim, it's getting curiouser and curiouser, like Alice in Wonderland, so guess what? I'll start a journal to note down all these fascinating episodes; what do you think?"

"Great idea, Vallo, and please remember to ask Orsina to add her observations; ok, ciao, Vallo."

The previous evening, as Valentino unlocked the front door of his apartment, the phone rang; he expecting a call from Orsina and was surprised to hear a very cultured ladies' voice, "Congratulations, Mr Valentino Cuccione, I am delighted to inform you that we would like to commission you to create a number of drawings and some oil paintings for one of our major clients; we hope you are able to accept this commission."

Valentino was stunned by this unexpected call and simply amazed by the news. After a few seconds, he said, "Yes madam. This sounds wonderful, and of course I accept the commission. But could you tell me who you are? What do you want me to draw and paint, and do I charge you my going rate?"

There was a brief chuckle at the other end of the phone before the caller's reply: "Mr Cuccione, you will start on an ongoing flat fee of one thousand dollars per week, starting on the day you confirm to me that you are ready to proceed. In addition, we will pay a generous fee for every single drawing and oil painting you complete. Arrangements will remain secret between us, and if you say yes, then you will receive instructions per telephone within twenty-four hours from now."

The Molehill

Valentino could not believe what he had heard he exclaimed, "Madam, this is fantastico, and yes, yes of course I accept. Thank you, thank you, very, very much."

That's when the phone went dead, but who cared? What wonderful news; he couldn't wait to tell Orsina when he met her at Grand Central Station on Friday evening.

Come on, Valentino, you are going to be rich, so let's bring on the special butiglia of Chianti Ruffino and Salute *to Mama, to Orsina, and to all our families. And I guess to the lovely lady who called and her big boss, whoever he is.*

Chapter 10

Central Park South: New York City

The park was still relatively quiet at this time of the morning, with few people strolling around at 07.15, but some energetic runners powered along the lanes as part of their early-morning workout. A group of local residents near the hotel practiced their tai chi on the lawn, and two riders galloped in pursuit along the path towards the woodland glade ahead.

Fenella Hardwick always enjoyed an early morning canter through the park, especially on such a beautiful day, where the mist had lifted and left the glow of morning due on the foliage of the trees, shrubs, and undergrowth. She had every reason to be happy, in many different ways: her thriving practice as a celebrated lawyer, based on her ability to analyse threats to her clients and to protect them from organized crime. But there was another reason why she felt ecstatic on this day.

She inhaled the crisp, fresh air and felt exhilarated by riding through the park; she looked forward to another exciting day. She smiled at the thought of how perfect her forthcoming, outbound break in the wilderness of Colorado would help her to relax, unwind and enjoy the solitude of the mountains. Little did Fenella know that just over four thousand miles away, north of Bologna in Italy, the plans for her Colorado adventure were already known; they had been discussed and were the subject of a fiendish conspiracy.

Professionally, she had become an expert at isolating those subversive elements that now and again tried their vicious tactics to discredit a company. This being part of their task, of preparing the ground for predators that forever seemed to circle successful businesses like vultures in readiness to pounce at the slightest sign of weakness.

Fenella's penthouse apartment at Central Park South was a perfect location for her business; it included lavishly furnished offices and fully equipped meeting rooms. It was the ideal location for her in this wealthy area of the town and not far away from Wall Street, where dynamic business deals were the order of the day.

Linked to this functional environment was her elegant personal apartment, which included luxurious accommodations for her guests, a roof garden, a swimming pool, and all together an oasis, where she was able to relax and unwind after her customary twelve-hour day (often much longer when business deals were at stake).

It was a day of celebration for Fenella, who was elated about her success the previous day, when one of her favourite clients, Rolf Brenner Inc, secured a further acquisition, this time in Louisville, Kentucky. This highly successful English company had established a subsidiary in Chicago several years ago and had become the target of a ruthless predator, who stopped at nothing, even criminal activities, to acquire RB Inc's offices, factories, and most of all their expertise.

Just under two years ago, a series of sinister activities including threats to individuals connected with Rolf Brenner Limited in England and RB Inc in the United States had developed into an international spider's web of intrigue, arson, kidnap, and murder. The perpetrators were eventually overwhelmed and eliminated; many were arrested or simply disappeared, gone to ground as a result of the resolute response from international law enforcement authorities.

These attacks were rebuffed thanks to the superb collaboration among officers from Scotland Yard, MI5, the Swiss Secret Service, a young and gifted NYPD lieutenant, and a retired US chief of police. Their exemplary way of rebuffing these attacks, of collaborating and overwhelming the opposition had since become a case study known as the Spider's Web Incident, debated in many academies as an exemplary model of counteracting and defeating organized crime.

Fenella had a significant role in outmanoeuvring these subversive activities, and she did so in close collaboration with Sir Nigel, now Lord Britton, an aristocrat with his home in England and one of the most creative and experienced financial experts in the world. His Lordship was a close associate of Rolf Brenner Ltd, RB Inc, and their transportation company in Dallas. He was also Fenella's close friend, and the thought of his arrival by Concorde later this morning filled her with joy and a tingle of anticipation.

This pleasant tingle was further accentuated by the movement of Renegade, her stallion, who was now powering down the slope to the little stream at the bottom of the hill. Breathing deeply and savouring the sensation of movement, she was riding on a wave of utter bliss for a short while, until Maria, her riding companion (and also her creative personal assistant and personal trainer), caught up with her.

"Hi boss, you simply look radiant this morning," the young woman said, smiling. "Do you know how fast you were going the last two miles?"

They both slowed down and let their horses change to a trot, proceeding leisurely along the path towards the park exit.

Wilson, one of Fenella's domestic staff, took care of the horses, and the doorman saluted as the two ladies entered the impressive and lavishly furnished lobby of the magnificent building at Central Park South.

As they approached the elevators near the reception area, a pageboy approached Fenella and said, "Good morning, Miss Hardwick, and sorry to bother you, ma'am, but this is for you." He presented her with an envelope on a silver salver.

"Thank you, Jimmy. I see it is addressed to be presented to me in person, so well done." She discreetly placed a five-dollar bill onto the tray and caught up with Maria, just as she was about to enter the elevator.

"How nice," she said to her assistant in the elegant lobby of her apartment, having opened the envelope. "It's from Nigel, signalled by the first officer from the Concorde flight deck of BA 001, now halfway across the Atlantic. Guess what he says?"

"Knowing him, a mixture of business, humour, affection, and a dinner date, perhaps?"

The Molehill

"Clever girl, Maria, you are spot on. This is what he says: 'ETA on time, meet you at the Pierre, can't wait, missed you, need your help re strange object, dinner at eight?'"

"Better get ready, Miss Hardwick," Maria said. "He is landing at 10.00, he should be in his suite by 11.15. I bet your pulse is already racing with the thought of this handsome, distinguished, and charming Lord of the Realm."

In the meantime, not far away from the park, Raymond Kenny, a young police officer, was in his element at the local NYPD district precinct, which covered the prestigious and wealthy surroundings near Central Park and Wall Street. His Irish parents had emigrated from the Emerald Isle; they settled in Boston, prospered, and provided Ray, his two brothers, and his sister with an excellent education.

His successful career in the force started at the police academy, where he graduated with honours, followed by three years as a rooky officer in one of the toughest law enforcement environments of Chicago. This was where the legendary police commissioner, Edward Pregowski, spotted the young officer's potential and offered him an appointment to his specialist team in Manhattan.

Ray loved the challenge of the NYPD; he was soon identified for fast-track development and was promoted to sergeant after only two years. On this early Thursday morning, he was at his desk in the lower Manhattan precinct. The lively environment around his desk was buzzing, and the officers who had been on duty during the night were signing off, completing the records about their shift, and handing things over to the bright-eyed and bushy-tailed team who now looked forward to the excitement of a new day. Some would be on foot patrol, others cruising in their squad cars, and some of them handling investigations and administrative duties in the office.

Sergeant Kenny was about to complete his report after a relatively quiet night, except for one sinister and as yet unexplained incident. There had been the usual minor disturbances that had been handled as a matter of routine. There were a few arrests for fighting in public, domestic violence, drunk and disorderly, and a couple of burglars who were caught in flagrante delictum.

Ray was glad that highway and traffic infringements did not fall under his jurisdiction; they were handled by a special department of the force, but when needed, they worked in collaboration with his boss, Lieutenant Leroy Simmons, and the men and women on the beat.

The other incident started with a call from a squad car on patrol in one of the more affluent roads of the town, not far away from the NYPD HQ. It was a quiet and select area of Manhattan, where elegant old houses lined the avenue. There appeared to be a problem in number 42; the front door was wide open, and there was some smoke coming out of it. The two officers spotted the wide-open door and immediately stopped their car; they radioed for backup, called for the fire services, and asked for another squad car to cover the back of the building in order to block any escape routes, just in case.

They cautiously made their way up the steps and entered the building, their weapons drawn; they were met with total silence and only a minimum of smoke. There was no sign of fire. The entrance hall looked spotless, totally undisturbed; it was lavishly furnished, and the wide, winding staircase did not indicate any evidence of a problem.

Backup arrived, and the team of four officers covered the ground floor salon, the dining room, the cloakroom, and the kitchen. Everything was in perfect order, and as the cellar door was locked, the officers decided to leave this area for later. The sounds of a fire engine announced the arrival of the brigade, but their chief was asked to hold off until the police officers had investigated, dealt with any challenges, and secured the upper floors of the house.

As they silently crept up the wide, sweeping staircase, they identified a light smell of smoke but no other indication of serious damage. They turned the corner, and when they entered the drawing room, they recoiled, shocked at the sight: An elderly man and woman were tightly tied to chairs in an upright position, with their lips sealed with tape. There was also some evidence of torture; the victims had then been suffocated.

There were two more bodies in the servants' area; a man and woman were found hanging from a ceiling beam by a rope, with their hands tied behind their backs. The intruders obviously wanted to dispose of witnesses, but silently and without attracting attention.

The Molehill

One of the upstairs rooms held a safe; the safe had been blown up, and it was empty. There was no sign of the perpetrators, and as a result, a major murder investigation began.

In the meantime, Ray completed his report and started to reflect. He was confident, of course, that the sophisticated machinery of the investigators and their teams would be successful and apprehend the perpetrators. But as he recalled a similar incident from quite some time ago, he wondered if there might be a connection with today's dreadful events. Deep in thought, he started making notes on the squared pad in front of him. Something about the incident had triggered a distant memory, including a name, the Cockney Demons, that was linked to a series of crimes about eighteen months earlier.

"Hi, Ray," chirped a cheerful voice behind his desk, as Sergeant Lara Pregowski placed a steaming mug of coffee in front of him and proceeded to add a couple of freshly prepared bagels and a jam doughnut.

"Lara, you are a sparkling star, as always," Ray said, chuckling at the young policewoman, who now perched on the corner of his desk, dangling her long and shapely legs, sipping from a steaming paper cup, and munching an apple.

"So, what's up, Ray? Why the furrowed brow on this lovely sunny morning? And what on earth are these funny squiggles you have drawn on your pad?"

Sergeant Kenny smiled at the young woman, mid-twenties, with chestnut hair tied in a flirty ponytail; her cheeky smile and twinkling dark brown eyes made her the picture of youthful energy and enthusiasm.

"Plenty for you to do, Lara," Ray said. "We've had a nasty multiple murder just a few blocks away from here, and one or two of the details remind me of the Cockney Demons you tackled so brilliantly quite some time ago."

"Now, that's just great, Ray. Thanks, but I thought we got rid of that scum when they were last on the scene."

"Anyway, guess we had better go and brief the boss. He should have landed at La Guardia by now; he took the red-eye from San Francisco after his conference speech about organized crime."

Kurt Hafner

"All in hand, Lara, and yes, Lieutenant Simmons had a car meet him at the airport; he should be here within half an hour, so let's review the details. Take a close look at the TCD files and make sure we receive regular updates from the investigating team."

Chapter 11

The Delivery: Southwest Florida

Samantha Townsend felt refreshed and contented on this lovely morning and so fortunate about the way her life was now developing, after several difficult years, including her failed relationships and the times she thought she'd never succeed in anything. This was despite her early achievements at St Andrews, a renowned private school where she excelled during her teens with outstanding grades.

After four years at college, she studied at the prestigious Norland Academy, where she graduated with flying colours as a fully trained nanny. She was elated when she donned her smart brown uniform with the pert hat and snow-white gloves, to take up her first appointment at the London home of a solicitor and his wife, who worked for one of the major banks.

This first appointment provided Samantha with a splendid start to her career. She loved the three children in her care, was appreciated by her employers, and continued to progress during those early years in her chosen profession. Her job meant everything to her and also helped her to forget the failed relationships with two early boyfriends, who had severely dented her confidence. At the time, she wondered whether she'd ever achieve anything. Those negative thoughts had now completely disappeared.

Following her twenty-ninth birthday, after seven years with her employers, she felt confident, in control of her destiny, and ready to move on to pastures new. In the meantime, the children in her care had also reached the right age to move on to boarding school; this was the perfect time for her to leave the townhouse in Kensington, review her options, and formulate her plans for the future, including an opportunity to broaden her horizons, ideally to see other parts of the world and, yes, to look for excitement and enjoy life.

Soon after her return to her parents' home, she was presented with the opportunity that she had been looking for, which was to take on the post of a nanny, with additional responsibilities of the children's education and running of the household. Sabine Brenner, who was a driving force and joint owner with her husband Rolf of a specialist electronics company, was looking for just such a young woman, and Samantha was delighted when she was offered the job.

What particularly attracted Samantha to her new appointment, which seemed like a dream come true, was the opportunity to travel. At the interview, she was informed her new employers lived with their two children in Hampshire but regularly stayed at their apartment in southwest Florida; they travelled to New York, Dallas, and Chicago, in addition to Sabine's native Germany and to Switzerland, France, and Italy.

So life was good with Samantha's arrival at Sabine and Rolf's home, not far away from their head office and specialist factory. All these positive elements proved to be the beginning of a rewarding appointment and a perfect step towards a successful future. Samantha soon managed to create her own style of contributing to the running of the old stately home; she gained the affection of the children, the respect of the staff, and the trust and appreciation of Rolf and Sabine.

So here was Sam, on the beach of a barrier island, increasing her pace and pounding through the sand, which was quite wet and heavy on the tread along the stretch just beyond the pier. This part of the beach was relatively quiet, except for the group of herons, egrets, and the occasional ibis that gathered on the old pier, which was always so lively with regular fishermen and visiting vacationers. As ever, there were a few holidaymakers on this quiet stretch of the beach, trying to catch some fish, and a few people bent over with what is called the Sanibel Stoop, looking for shells.

The Molehill

There were also some isolated residents and visitors, who decided to extend their run along this more isolated part of the shore, including the two runners, who were now rapidly approaching, just as Samantha started to slow down, ready to reach the low wall in front of one of the other resorts. She normally sat here for a while, soaking up the beauty of the surroundings, enjoying a few moments of reflection, before preparing for her final spurt on her return to her resort.

This was where the incident happened: In the shrubbery along the sand, the two runners appeared and blocked her progress, then created enough space for her to pass; as she went by, they nudged her, and she stumbled, tried to regain her balance, but slipped down the low bank onto the moist sand, where she sat dazed for a few minutes.

"You bastards!" she shouted, but the two of them were already far away and had almost reached the pier.

She brushed herself down, took a large gulp of Dasani water from her bottle, grinned ruefully, and approached the wall, where she sat for a while, cooling off. She started to see the funny side of the episode, except for the flash in the bushes, that played on her mind.

Not very long, though, because her ebullient personality and a mischievous sense of humour soon restored her high spirits, and her combative mood empowered her to accelerate, increase her pace, and reach the beach in front of the resort in record time. She gradually slowed her pace, cooling down after her run, stretching her limbs, soaking up the view, briefly basking in the sun, and then gradually strolling towards the entrance to the boardwalk, which led up to the swimming pool and the beautifully kept grounds, with the apartment blocks situated beyond.

At poolside, she met some of the other residents, who had already settled at the tables under the umbrellas; they chatted underneath the shady pergola or enjoyed an early morning swim. Samantha decided to cool off in the water and proceeded to swim twelve powerful lengths, before changing to a more leisurely stroke.

"Hi, Sammy; how are you, chick?" a cheerful voice suddenly called out from the poolside. "Just coming in for a chat with you because guess what? That weird guy in 6B keeps on staring at me, but I guess he looks quite nice, don't you think?"

"G'day, Aussi Vicky, you look stunning as ever, and I am so glad your folks from down under settled in exotic Colorado."

The two young women teased each other for a while, comparing notes until it was time for Samantha to towel herself dry and complete a full set of her athletic stretches; after that she returned to her apartment to take a shower and dress for the day.

As Samantha walked across the courtyard later, she passed the office and noticed a courier delivering something to the manager. She wondered if it was for Sabine and Rolf.

In any case, Samantha needed to freshen up; she felt hungry and looked forward to a light breakfast with the family before their day out. As she reached the top of the stairs to 3C, she noticed an envelope in the wooden holder outside her apartment; she retrieved it, went inside, and placed it on the kitchen table.

Before opening the envelope, she went to the bathroom and took a luxurious shower, enjoying the pressure of the spray on her body and the warm sensation that gradually engulfed her, especially at the thought of those two muscular young men who had knocked her off the path. She started to fantasize what their true intention might have been, but just for a while, and then her annoyance about their aggressiveness returned, and she vowed to challenge them if they reappeared in future.

As she dried herself, she was pleased to see her image in the full-sized mirror, which showed her perfectly proportioned figure: small, pert breasts; slim waist; and long, shapely legs that complemented her athletic build. The original plain-Jane appearance of her early years had been replaced by a more mature and confident look, including her intelligent blue eyes under arched eyebrows, a slightly upturned nose, and full red lips, which contrasted with her long, brown hair, which she normally wore in a ponytail.

She looked forward to her day; Rolf and Sabine planned to drive with their children, James and Sophie, and her along the coast and then to amble down as far as Naples with all its lovely boutiques, attractions, children's facilities, and fine eateries.

Samantha chose a short denim skirt with a wide, dark blue belt and a tight-fitting blouse with a crisp blue, lemon, and white check pattern;

The Molehill

she applied a small amount of makeup, added a splash of Miss Dior, picked up her mobile and shoulder bag, and was just about to leave when she remembered the envelope on the kitchen table. It was addressed "To Sam" and contained a folded piece of paper with a drawing of a Norland Nanny's hat, laying upside down on a sandy beach. Underneath was written in block letters "WE ARE WATCHING YOU AND YOUR EMPLOYERS." Nothing else.

Samantha grew angry at the threat. *How dare they, whoever they are?* she thought; was it a prank, or was it a serious message for her, Sabine, and Rolf? Was it connected to the flash in the shrubbery during her morning run and the two ruffians who pushed her off the path?

She brewed herself a strong cup of coffee with an additional shot of espresso, sat on the lanai, and reflected on the unusual events of the morning and this strange note, wondering what to do. After a while, she felt more comfortable, and her logical mind, combined with her ever-present sense of humour, helped her see the funny side of what had happened. She also made up her mind that she would not mention anything to Rolf and Sabine, at least not at this stage, as she did not want anything to affect what promised to be a most enjoyable and pleasant day for the five of them.

She relaxed for a while, and in truth, the memory of the morning's mini dramas made her smile. Soon, she closed her apartment door and locked it, skipped down the stairs, and joined the family for a Florida orange juice and a bowl of granola. They were all in high spirits; Rolf positioned the car and was ready for their departure.

They were on the way, taking a leisurely drive along the coast road, past Fort Myers Beach, to Estero, where they stopped at Perkins for a substantial breakfast and to recharge their batteries. They continued in the direction of Naples, spending some time in the popular boutiques on the way. They also stopped and allowed the children to play in the sand; after a while, they continued their journey to Tin City. They were fond of this charming and unique conglomeration of quaint little shops, and after browsing and making a few purchases, they relaxed at the Waterside Restaurant for a while and enjoyed a delicious lunch, before proceeding to the Coastland Mall.

They looked forward to admiring the wonderful sculptures of eagles, herons, waders, dolphins, and turtles that were so tastefully displayed in the special area just inside the main entrance. They strolled around the many tempting stores, and the children were allowed to browse in the toy departments, the bookstores, and the entertainment store, where they selected some DVDs and CDs to add to their growing collection.

Sabine and Samantha did a spot of window-shopping, before deciding what items to buy in addition to their already substantial list of dresses, shoes, gadgets, and many other goods they were planning to purchase.

Rolf, in the meantime, positioned himself on a bench outside the mall; he was making phone calls to his head office in UK and also his subsidiaries in Chicago and Atlanta. Business was brisk, but there were concerns about the share price, which for unknown reasons kept losing ground. Nigel Britton was on the case, of course, and due in New York in order to team up with Fenella Hardwick, his brilliant USA lawyer. Having made a few more notes in his journal, Rolf started to relax; he watched the many different people who arrived and those who left the mall, laden with their purchases.

At that moment, he heard a sound that became progressively louder, and then he spotted a group of bikers, who were roaring around the square with increasing tempo and plenty of noise. They were wearing green bandanas adorned by a black emblem; green scarves shielded their faces but did not stop their screaming shrieks and howls.

Their manoeuvres progressively became more focused on the area where Rolf stood, observing the spectacle in front of him. The six bikers suddenly formed into a column and roared past Rolf; the last rider dropped an envelope at his feet, and they left the area, hooting, screaming, and disappearing around the corner.

Some people going to the mall watched the strange spectacle of the bikers; they shook their heads and quietly dispersed, whilst Rolf carefully examined the envelope and finally decided to open it. There was a white card with a printed message: "Beware, you are all in mortal danger. Sell your company, and live peacefully ever after."

Rolf reflected for a while and considered his options. He was quite certain subversive elements were once again threatening his family and their business. Their goal seemed to be the acquisition of Rolf Brenner Limited, RB Inc, and their subsidiary in Dallas. Well, they were picking on the wrong organization; the family had both resources and connections to thwart any criminal activity. He decided to discuss the incident at the mall and the written warning with his close friend, Edward Pregowski, who was a legendary retired chief of police; he owned one of the apartments on the resort.

He met up with his troops in the coffee shop, they stowed their purchases in the car and headed for a delicious seafood dinner at the Red Lobster. After eating, they headed down Interstate 41 and returned to their resort.

It turned out to be a lively finish to a perfect day, and with the children already in bed, an enjoyable evening with drinks and snacks on the lanai. Their relaxation, however, ended the moment Rolf, Sabine and Samantha made a dramatic and sinister discovery.

Chapter 12

Interstate 678: New York

Concorde swooped down, and passengers on the right side of the aircraft were treated to a magnificent view of Manhattan's famous skyline, before BA 001 gently swooped down like a giant bird and majestically touched down on the runway. Thereafter followed just a short wait as the magnificent aircraft taxied to the gate, where the reception committee of managers, BA special services, operations controllers, ground crew, and porters were waiting to contribute to a smooth and seamless service on arrival.

The observer carefully followed the flight path with her binoculars from a nearby building, and as the aircraft touched down, she signalled her colleague, who would now take up her position within the terminal, whilst Nelson was ready to move on command.

"Welcome to New York, my Lord," Special Services Agent Courtney said, as she escorted Nigel Britton towards the terminal. "Did you have a pleasant flight?'"

"Splendid as always," Nigel said; "comfortable journey, delicious food, and perfect attention by Kathryn and her crew."

"So glad, and you arrived right on schedule."

"Yes, Captain Richards got us here, bang on time. So what's the form now, my dear? What have you organized for me today?"

"Just a smooth transition to your limo; Parker is waiting on the starting grid. This way, sir. Hank is already loading your luggage into the trunk. And sir, this special message was delivered by hand a while ago." She handed Nigel a sealed white envelope.

"Thank you, Courtney; how very nice," Britton said with a twinkle in his eye. "Perhaps I'll see you when I check in for my return flight after my holiday in Colorado?"

"I'll make sure to be here, my Lord. We all wish you a lovely break in the mountains." The young agent handed Nigel to her colleague who would see him safely through Customs before his journey to the Pierre Hotel in Manhattan.

As the elegant and distinguished aristocrat left the terminal with his security escort, two of the flight attendants were watching and comparing notes about Lord Britton.

"Wow, Sinead, what style," Helen crooned. "And did you notice those eyes and the way he looks at you?"

"I know," Sinead said, "and he lives not far away from us at Rushdown Hall."

As the two young women continued their analysis, they were not the only eyes watching Lord Britton.

Nearby, the observer's sharp binoculars had been focused on Nigel Britton ever since he appeared behind the glass portal of the terminal and then followed his every movement until he settled in the car. Several photographs were taken of him and particularly the limo and then sent by a coded signal to Nelson, the man known as the Operator.

While Nigel's car took the Van Wyck Expressway, he read the note from his close friend and business associate, Fenella Hardwick, the glamorous and celebrated lawyer. Her large, expressive handwriting made him smile, as he read, "Good morning, your Lordship, and welcome to the colonies (So sorry). Can't meet you until this evening, RB issues; surprising but very exciting. Old times? Just my cup of tea. Tell you later, CP South at 8pm? I'll be starving, and really, really hungry."

Nigel smiled as his limousine passed La Guardia Airport, then Flushing Meadows, the world-famous site of the US Open Tennis Championship. He was glad, in a way, that his luncheon date was cancelled; like Fenella, he was dealing with concerns about Rolf Brenner Ltd, Rolf Brenner Inc, and their transportation outfit in Dallas.

Following the incidents about eighteen months ago, the company had rebounded but all of a sudden seemed to have stalled. A number of negative messages had caused a steady decline in share prices. A hostile raid of Rolf Brenner Inc was imminent. Nigel felt fired up about the challenges ahead for him, for Fenella, and for their brilliant teams. As he thought about this, he noticed an enormous, shiny truck in the next lane of the expressway; it travelled at great speed and all of a sudden veered closer to his limo.

Parker had noticed the truck and announced calmly, "Right, sir, action stations, and here goes."

He immediately accelerated and escaped the threat of a serious collision. The way ahead was relatively clear, with just a few vehicles on their way to the city, and the commando-trained driver would normally have sped away and put some distance between his car and the idiot truck driver. Was he drunk, on drugs, or was there a more sinister purpose behind his intentions?

The powerful truck reappeared and repeated his attempt to squeeze the limo against the outer wall of the expressway. Nigel caught a glimpse of a grinning red face as the passenger in the truck raised his hand and pointed a handgun at his target.

As all hell broke loose, they approached one of the bridges, and the freeway just further ahead; a collision seemed inevitable. Suddenly, a police helicopter hovered overhead and then dropped nail-studded planks in front of the truck, which came to a sudden stop. The driver's cab was now surrounded by police, who had spilled from a pursuing car. At the same time, five uniformed motorcyclists swarmed from behind and sandwiched the vehicle.

"Go, go, go," one of the police officers called out to Parker, waving him on, as the driver accelerated and elegantly bypassed the ugly scene to his left.

Nigel took a last look at the receding scenario and was quite certain he recognized one of the faces within the police contingent. And as if on cue, his cell phone rang. A cheerful voice said, "Good morning, Lord Britton, glad to be of service. Best wishes from all of us at the NYPD."

"Sergeant Pregowski, how nice and comforting to hear your voice,

The Molehill

my dear. Can't thank you enough for dealing with that problem. My compliments to all of you and kind regards to Lieutenant Simmons."

"You're welcome, sir. Good luck with RB."

Nigel smiled at the thought of this energetic and talented young police sergeant. He made a few mental notes about what he had seen, and the limo soon entered Manhattan after crossing the Verrazano Bridge, and a few minutes later, the uniformed concierge of the Pierre opened the door of the car.

"Welcome, Lord Britton," he said, bowing lightly as Nigel entered the hotel lobby.

Normally, Lord Britton would have changed into his sports gear and gone for a run in the park, then luxuriated in his bath before enjoying a light lunch in the restaurant, tended by Francois, the maître d', who was an expert in gauging the wishes of his special customers. Today, though, Nigel started with the up-to-date information about the day's financial markets, watching the latest news from Wall Street on the giant screen in his suite and making a number of telephone calls to mobilize his troops.

He asked Francois to book dinner for two at one of the latest culinary hotspots in town and then took a close look at the documents that were annotated with his trademark green notes, arrows, balloons, and stars. He looked pleased, as he carefully placed the documents into plastic sleeves of several colours and into his Tumi executive bag.

Then he stepped closer to the remaining item on the table, the mysterious envelope that had been delivered to Rolf and Sabine Brenner at their head office in England, a few days earlier. He carefully placed the document into the secure safe of his suit. He briefly checked his appearance, called the concierge to arrange for Parker to bring the car around, and made his way to the lobby with a spring in his step.

A few blocks away from the Pierre, Fenella Hardwick's business suite was a hive of activity. She was in her element, assisted by Maria, a Stanford graduate who responded to her clipped commands with precision. Patrick, a brilliant young lawyer, had proved to be a perfect addition to the team; he specialized in dealing with rumours and innuendo involved in the effort to discredit the company. The evidence gradually pointed to an as-yet-unknown organization that were preparing a raid on Rolf Brenner's businesses both in England and in the United States.

The raider was trying to discredit the company and therefore lower the share price; damaging and false stories had been leaked to the media. Some of these had since started to appear in the business publications and were thereafter being mentioned on the radio and on television.

The information being collated had already grown into a sizeable portfolio. Fenella smiled and told Patrick, "Remember the Spider's Web Incident, eighteen months ago? Well, today's pattern is similar to what preceded those dramatic events. Let us just hope that what we are dealing with now is nothing more than a storm in a teacup, as my English friends would say."

"'Hope you are right, Miss Hardwick," Patrick said. "There will be no criminal activities and violence ahead of us like last time."

As if on cue, the internal telephone rang; Maria answered and said, "Miss Hardwick, Lieutenant Simmons is in the lobby and would like to speak to you."

"That may just be a signal of possible trouble; ask the lieutenant to join me in the roof garden."

Fenella grew pensive but remained smiling. She was tall and elegant in her tailored Chanel suit, which accentuated her perfect figure as she mounted the top floor of her apartment.

Within a few minutes, the lieutenant emerged from the elevator and was met by Maria, who escorted him up the stairs into the roof garden, where Fenella had taken her seat in the gazebo. She wore hardly any makeup and did not really need it, on account of her beautiful olive-coloured skin, which suggested the possibility of a partial and distant ancestry related to the original inhabitants of the United States. She wore her jet black hair in a stylish knot at the nape of her neck, which accentuated her almond-shaped dark eyes and her expressive eyebrows.

As the lieutenant approached, she glanced at him with a mischievous smile, shook hands, and said, "Welcome and tell me, what exciting news brings you here today?"

"Plenty, Miss Hardwick, and yes, intriguing developments for my troops to pursue. Some of them impact your current investigations."

"So let's have it; what's up?"

"First of all, we increased surveillance of yourself and your connections after we identified suspicious signals from the underworld. Lord Britton landed on time at JFK and, as you will have heard, was faced with some difficulties on the journey to the Pierre. I am glad to say he is currently on Wall Street and of course we are keeping a discreet guard on him at all times."

Simmons described the incident that had occurred on the way into Manhattan and reassured Fenella that his team had handled the situation; he also outlined measures now in place to counteract any subversive activities.

The young lieutenant said, "Miss Hardwick, I'd like to make you aware of another matter that is related to your current activities with Rolf Brenner Inc. This concerns one of the major investors who had pledged to make a substantial investment in the company, in order to allow the business to expand further in the United States.

"I am sorry to inform you that Mr and Mrs Robertson and some of their staff were murdered at their home early yesterday morning. We are handling this crime as a failed break-in; however, we do have evidence to suggest there are wider implications, some of which will undoubtedly cause damage to your clients."

"Thank you for your precise and frank presentation of the facts," Fenella said. "Half an hour ago, I was saying to my team there are hints of what became known as the Spider's Web Incident eighteen months ago and perhaps even indications of the Cockney Demons, the criminal gang we eliminated, but who knows?"

"Miss Hardwick, you are as perceptive as ever; we are ready to tackle the problems head-on."

"Thank you, Lieutenant. I guess it's time to go into battle for you and your troops, for Nigel Britton and his team, and for my organization. Yippee, happy days," she said with a stubborn, determined look on her face.

Chapter 13

The Task: New York

It was a brilliant sunny morning in Queens; Valentino Cuccione was pensive as he sat on the balcony of his apartment and sipped a double espresso. He was quite worried now, because there had been no contact, no news, and no instructions of what on earth his mysterious employer wanted him to produce. What drawings would he be asked to create? Which oil painting might he be expected to put on canvas?

Sure enough, he was absolutely elated after the unexpected and mysterious telephone caller; the woman had told him, in a cultured American accent with a slight Southern twang, that he would be paid a retainer of one thousand dollars per week, irrespective of any work he was instructed to produce. This was several days ago.

The voice had also said he would be paid a generous fee for every single drawing or painting he created. The next morning, the voice called again to say he would receive instructions at a secret location.

"*Porco Dio, sinistra, brutto maiale,*" he swore as he paced the floor; he kicked the armchair, banged his fist on the kitchen worktop, and shouted, "*Malafecto, bastardos,*" out of the window, followed by a stream of further expletives. Then, almost as if on cue, his cell phone rang; it was a junior bank manager, asking to speak to Mr Valentino Cuccione.

"Just a courtesy call, sir," he said, "to confirm that your weekly income of one thousand dollars is accumulating, and we are awaiting your instruction about your possible wishes for the funds to be invested."

Valentino quickly regained his composure after the initial elation of

The Molehill

the news and replied nonchalantly. "Yes, I was awaiting your call," he said. "Better late than never, I suppose. You will receive instructions about my investment plans soon, goodbye." Then he roared with laughter, burst into song, and enjoyed himself for about an hour, planning how he would surprise and delight Orsina on her arrival in less than twenty-four hours.

It was soon time to change into his formal manager's attire and make his way to the restaurant. He looked forward to being in control of the business this afternoon and especially the evening. There was an exciting event scheduled in the first-floor conference suite, starting with an important meeting of senior captains of industry in addition to their lawyers, bankers, and advisors. This was then to be followed by cocktails and a lavish dinner prepared by a famous celebrity chef and his team.

There was a real buzz on his arrival; staff were visibly fired up and determined to put on a superb show for this prestigious event. Business was still quite brisk at this time of day, with late lunchtime guests enjoying their meal and others drifting in for refreshments or a beverage.

The couple in the corner near the window looked somewhat familiar to Valentino, but he paid no attention to them, as he wanted to check the event's progress. He inspected the first-floor cloakroom, the meeting room for the twenty-four guests, the anteroom for the reception, and most of all, the special room where the meal was to be served; the celebrity chef and his team had already started preparations in the kitchen.

He was pleased to see the assistant managers had done well, and everything was progressing according to plan. On his way downstairs to inspect the kitchen and service areas, he passed the attractive lady he had noticed in the corner; she wore a summer dress, and the gentleman she was with wore a formal suit. She was on her way to the upstairs cloakrooms, which was a more discreet area for guests to freshen up.

"Mr Cuccione," the young receptionist called, "here's the latest printout of the guest list, which now includes the mayor and the sheriff."

"Good girl, Miranda, many thanks. Glad you've got it under control; I want you to help me greet our guests as they arrive."

The woman he passed on the stairs went into a cloakroom cubicle, opened her large soft designer handbag, and extracted a restaurant server's uniform; she slipped it easily over her dress. Her bag also held a large cardboard perfume presentation box, which she deftly disguised in the small pile of linen napkins that were at the base of her bag. Now empty, she flattened it, folded it, and then placed into her uniform's large pocket.

She left the cloakroom, checked the surroundings, and then marched confidently into the service area, carrying a pile of table linen. She went past the kitchen staff and into the deserted dining room, which was in semi-darkness. The table was beautifully dressed and edged by an elegant valance. One of the junior waiters walked in, startling her. She busied herself by folding napkins; he smiled at her and said, "Hi there, the room looks wonderful. See you later." He disappeared through the door into the service area.

After completing her final task, the woman returned via the reception area and the conference room; she made her way to the cloakroom and soon emerged in her original attire, carrying her handbag. She gracefully descended the stairs and joining her companion, who had remained at their table and was busy reading the *Wall Street Journal* and the *Financial Times*.

"Busy as ever, I see," she sneered, "and where is your master plan for Cuccione, if you please? Don't tell me you have not even made a start. Whereas my mission is accomplished, of course, no snags, no problems, and no one got in the way. A highly professional job, as always, my dear. Exactly as I have been directed by our section chief on behalf of the Almighty One."

"Shut up, Elna, you cheeky little minx. I have also been busy, passed a few more messages to some of the news editors, which should put the cat amongst the pigeons. I also found the perfect place to brief Cuccione about what our chief directed us to produce."

"Sounds promising, Christopher, but bloody well don't cock it up again."

The man just smiled, finished his glass of Californian merlot, and said, "Come on now, you spiky little cow, I've already paid, so let's go."

They left the restaurant and strolled down the road to their very special destination.

Meanwhile, the restaurant had become a hive of activity, and as

The Molehill

the tempo increased, Valentino was in his element. He changed into formal attire and monitoring progress, inspected the function rooms, and reassured the celebrity chef and his crew that everything was ready to do justice to their delicious creations.

Valentino then went into top gear, and in order to do so, he needed truly inspirational music; no, not Pavarotti, he decided, but the tunes that inspired him in Gstaad, Switzerland, where he was a junior commis waiter at the famous Royal Palace Hotel one summer and winter season. So "Volare, Volare," "Arrividerci Roma," and many others started to enhance the background of Italy.

Valentino stopped himself from blaring out the songs, but contented himself by humming them happily as he went about his business. "*Ciao, bella Biondina,*" he told Ashley, as he passed her on the stairs. She was balancing a large tray of salt and pepper cellars; she had filled them, but not right to the top, as some of her untrained colleagues tended to do, which prevented diners from seasoning their meals.

As she reached the top of the stairs, she broke into a little jig to the Italian tune, waltzing along the corridor and dreaming about Valentino holding her in his arms, looking at her with his smouldering dark eyes, giving her breasts a cheeky squeeze, and making her feel full of warmth and pleasure.

"Come on, you dumb blonde, get a move on," a shout from the senior waiter brought her back to earth. "Hurry up and complete dressing the table; it should have been done half an hour ago."

"Yes sir, Mr Bluit, sorry about the delay, but look how perfectly I followed your guidance with those cellars, which are almost but not quite full?"

"Not too bad, I suppose," Bluit grumbled, as he grudgingly inspected the condiment holders. "Come on, girl, we are running out of time, so just shift it, and do it right now."

Ignoring his petulant shout, Ashley stalked off in the direction of the service area; she stuck her tongue out and hissed, "Piss off, you stupid fat prick," which made her feel a lot better and even more so, as the soothing, romantic Italian tune now put her into a lovely mellow mood, just ready to complete her task.

As she skipped into the dining room and towards the table, she accidentally tripped over some napkins that had been carelessly left near the base of the service table. One of the saltcellars dropped from her tray, fell to the floor, and rolled underneath the table.

"Oh, darn," she said but dutifully carried on with her task of placing the elegant cellars; she stood back to admire her work and then crouched down to retrieve the missing saltcellar. As it was nowhere to be seen, she lifted the valance that edged the table and crawled underneath it to locate the missing condiment.

Despite the semi-darkness, she spotted another untidy pile of linen napkins and was puzzled as to why they should have been placed underneath the table; she decided to gather them up into a neat pile for her colleagues in the service area. As she did, she noticed something hard placed in between the napkins and to her delight saw it was a perfume box, featuring one of the most prestigious and exclusive brands available in the superb establishments of Fifth Avenue.

First of all, she completed the table by adding the last condiment cellar, then she smiled, gathered the box of perfumes, hugged it, and pretended dishy Mr Valentino was holding her in his arms as she slowly danced towards the service area.

Bluit, who had been watching the young girl, crept up behind her and hissed, "In your own little dream world again, are we, Miss Ashley? What is this, a box of perfume? Hand it to me right now, you devious little cow."

"No, Mr Bluit, this is a present from my boyfriend, who left it for me at reception."

"Rubbish, my girl," Bluit snapped. "Just hand it to me right now. I'll investigate this incident after the banquet tonight." He tried to wrench the box out of her hand.

He managed to do so and triumphantly shook the box in front of her eyes; there was a metallic click within the box, and then the world of Ashley and Bluit exploded with a loud detonation; the destructive blast tore their bodies to pieces.

There was a deafening silence for a few seconds, and then there was absolute chaos, screams from staff, who had been near the service area, mingled with agonizing sounds from the young waiter who lay badly

The Molehill

injured in the doorway to the kitchen. Downstairs, Valentino was dazed but managed to call the emergency services, and then he guided his staff to evacuate the guests from the restaurant, before dashing upstairs with his assistant manager. Within minutes, they could hear the sound of approaching sirens, police cars, ambulances, and fire engines, and soon the superb teams of all three services under the direction of NYPD Lieutenant Simmons swung into action, restoring a sense of order out of these tragic events.

The NYPD temporarily closed the premises and began a meticulous investigation into these tragic events, starting with a detailed analysis of the crime scene, including a complete list of all employees, the customers who had been on the premises, and particularly the guests who were due to attend the formal dinner later that day.

In the meantime, Valentino had arranged to transfer the banquet to the sister restaurant of his employers and personally contacted every single guest, reassuring them he personally would be there. Some of the key members of his team, who were still stunned by the tragedy of the events, had volunteered to join him to ensure the quality of the arrangements more than matched the new venue for this prestigious event.

Later that evening, as the guests comfortably reclined in their seats, enjoying a fine malt whiskey, premium aged bourbon, thirty-year-old Port, or some delicious liqueurs, the mayor rose to address those around the table. He started in a sombre mood by expressing the group's condolences to the families of the bereaved and offering sympathy to those who were injured and traumatized by the event.

"And now," he said, "we are all of us so immensely proud of the courage and dedication of Mr Valentino Cuccione and his staff, who dealt with the aftermath of this attack and, against all the odds, created a most wonderful evening."

As the mayor continued, he gave a rousing speech of defiance against any subversives, criminals, or terrorists who might be behind the attack at their original venue for this very special evening. He enthused about the speed and efficiency of the emergency services and also acknowledged the exemplary support of the staff of their relocated venue.

And in conclusion, he reassured all those present that Lieutenant Simmons, one of NYPD's most promising detectives, was on the case, and his team would not rest until the perpetrators of this heinous crime were brought to justice. He brought the evening to a close by announcing generous donations to the victims of the attack, to the NYPD, and to the emergency services that had been involved. Finally, he invited Valentino and his staff for a special reception that was being planned at the town hall in the near future.

What an incredible day, Valentino thought as he quietly walked along the avenue towards his apartment later that evening; first of all, the good news from the bank, then the excitement of the preparations for the evening and the tragic events; how sad about lovely little Ashley, and the shock of it all. Then the resilience, his creative solution to relocate, and finally, the triumph of a wonderful evening, with so many accolades for him and his staff.

As he trudged along the sidewalk, a motorbike roared alongside him; the rider, disguised by heavy leather gear and a scarf wrapped around his face, hissed, "Get in your car, wait for a phone call, and someone will direct you to the place where you will pick up the details of your task."

Although feeling quite exhausted after the excitement and trauma of the day, Valentino grew elated; he shouted, "Yes, yes, yes, at last I will be able to show my new boss what I can do."

He hurried to his apartment, where he changed into casual clothing, grabbed a briefcase, and picked up the keys of his ten-year-old sedan. He went outside and sat in his car and soon received a call on his cell phone. The voice directed him to drive left at the main road, then branch off with further instructions until he reached the desolate recycling area. He was told to stop in front of a dilapidated warehouse.

"Enter," the voice commanded, and as Valentino stepped through the door, he found himself in a corridor; he was told to walk along and take the first door on the right. He entered a cavernous hanger and saw a muffled figure wearing a fedora hat sitting at a desk on a stage.

"Welcome, Mr Cuccione," the man said in a cultured English voice, "and congratulations on your splendid performance today. Please understand that your connection with my organization, any

The Molehill

communications between us, and especially the work you are going to do will be strictly confidential. Any disclosure would have severe consequences for you and Orsina, so strict secrecy, if you please. But now for the good news: We are pleased to have you on board, and here is what I want you to create tomorrow. You'll be told where to deliver it and at what time.

"You will create three drawings for me, A5 in size, in charcoal on white background, and here is what the three images will portray." Valentino was delighted by two of the subjects but puzzled and somewhat uneasy about the third.

"Thank you, sir," he said. "The drawings will be ready for you. I shall await your instructions."

"Good man, Cuccione. I look forward to seeing your work, and if I am satisfied, I will arrange for you to be paid six thousand dollars for each of the three drawings. Now go and forget we ever met in this desolate place."

"*Fantastico*, fantastic," Valentino shouted as he drove home in his clapped-out Alfa Romeo. "I am going to be rich and spoil my Orsina when I meet her in two days' time." He was ecstatic with happiness, and yet, some nagging concern crept into his thoughts, turning his smile into a serious frown.

Chapter 14

Early Dawn: Southwest Florida

The day trip to Naples had been a perfect outing for Rolf and Sabine Brenner, their two children, and Nanny Samantha. Before returning home, they had a delicious dinner at Red Lobster; they were looking forward to a relaxing evening and a few cocktails on the lanai, once the children were asleep.

As lovely as this had been, Samantha was frightened about the threatening note; she hadn't disclosed it to Rolf and Sabine yet, nor had she mentioned the two louts who accosted her on the beach.

The causeway soon came into view, and the island beyond, with the full moon intermittently appearing in between heavy, dark clouds; the weather news predicted a threatening storm, which was expected to hit the coast the following day.

There was another storm brewing, however; Rolf and Sabine were furious about the harassment by the bikers and their naïve message, which angered the two of them. They formulated a plan to contact Edward Pregowski, retired NYPD commissioner and Rolf's international criminal and military specialists.

Once back in their apartment, it took quite a while to calm the children down as they re-enacted the mad pack of motorbikes they had seen through the main door of the mall. They turned into bikers, with bandanas, and James made himself a beard out of paper and a pretend ponytail. They made roaring noises, shrieking, as they ran around with each other, but they finally calmed down to eat another snack, drink some milk, and finally were ready for their shower and then to go to bed.

"OK, girls, let's get a round of drinks," Rolf said, and they all sat at the table on the lanai, having toasted a thoroughly enjoyable day, and started to chat. Sabine decided to take a look at the flat parcel that had been delivered that morning, just as they were leaving for the day's outing, along the coast.

"Let's have another drink," said Rolf, "and then let's open the mystery delivery." He carefully scrutinized the details on the package. It was simply addressed to RB Inc, with no further details; there was no indication about the sender.

"Right, here goes," said Rolf, as he carefully pulled at the seal of the large envelope. The contents were wrapped in yellow tissue paper, and the first thing they noticed were two thin leather strings.

Samantha giggled.

"What on earth?" exclaimed Sabine, but Rolf raised his hands, looked serious, and said, "Don't touch, whatever you do."

The women gasped as Rolf revealed the final exhibit in the shape of a small painting, about twelve inches by eight, showing a beautiful scenery of the beach starting with a close-up and then tapering into the distance. What made this painting sinister, however, was the image of a noose that was hanging in midair. There was one more object, a professional drawing that showed a saloon car with its passenger compartment being ripped apart by a violent explosion.

Samantha burst into tears, and as Sabine put her arms around her, she sobbed uncontrollably.

"What on earth has upset you, darling Sami?"

"Aw, Sabine, I am so, so sorry. I should have told you first thing, but oh, I didn't want to spoil our lovely day." Sobbing, she added, "I was attacked while running on the beach, and then, I received this nasty note in my mail."

"Don't you worry, Sami; you are such a star, and how brave of you to keep this nasty secret all day long because of your love for our family. Rolf and I have dealt with this in the past; we think we know who's behind it

Kurt Hafner

all, and we have all the necessary connections to snuff out these awful threats.

Rolf carefully scrutinized the collection of exhibits, held up his hand to stop anyone touching the objects, and immediately called Edward Pregowski, his neighbour and former chief of police. His lively wife, Phyllis, responded in a jiffy, as she would say.

"Now good evening, dear, whoever you are, and I guess you want to talk to my Edward, who is on the phone to Leroy Simmons, and you know how long they chat, those two, when they are talking about old times and even worse when they are comparing notes about a current criminal case."

"Darling Phyllis, how lovely to hear your bubbly, cheerful voice, and may I please ask for the chief to pop round and give me some advice about a fascinating collection of exhibits after he has spoken to Leroy?"

"Of course he will, dear Rolf, and please give my love to your lovely wife and lively children. I will send Edward with a large plate of my orange brownies, which I baked a while ago."

Shortly afterwards, Edward Pregowski arrived with a large plate of brownies, sparkling eyes, and a broad grin below his stylish moustache. "So come on, young Rolf, what's up? How may I be of help?" Half an hour later, Edward had mobilized the local chief of police, Joyce Allan, and her forensic team to examine the detail of the exhibits.

The following day, as dawn was breaking towards the east of the island, Samantha felt physically refreshed but emotionally subdued after their serious discussion, which lasted late into the evening. She always enjoyed her early mornings on the beach, and she suddenly thought, *Come on, Samantha, don't be such a wimp but liven up so go, go, go.* Soon after, she was stretching her limbs and warming up before setting off at a brisk pace down the beach in the direction of the pier. She wore her customary sports outfit of designer shorts, cropped top, and running shoes.

She was quite alone on the beach; she loved the solitude, peace, and quiet, which was only interrupted by the receding tide gently lapping across the sand, the occasional twirl of the waders flying in formation,

The Molehill

and the shrieks of the terns and gulls that populated various stretches of the sand at low tide.

After a while, she spotted a runner who was powering towards her; she recognized the tall, statuesque young lady, whom she had seen several times before. She was the same height and build as Samantha; she slowed down as she reached the long gradual bend, at the same time as Sam.

"Hi, there; how are you?" chirped the newcomer.

"Fine, thank you, and I am so impressed by your athletic running style."

"Well, that's Princeton for you. Wow, I just love your running gear; real cool."

"Yep, it's Burberry, my dear, but hey, I'm Sam, and I'm over here from England."

"You don't say," the young American girl said, smiling. "My name's Selina, born and bred in Dayton, Ohio."

As the two girls strolled towards the recreation area just off the beach, they continued chatting, telling each other about their background, comparing notes about boyfriends, and exchanging their experience of recent weird happenings along the beach. Sam told Selena about the flash photography that had startled her the previous morning and then the two men who had pushed her off the path.

"I called them stupid jerks, and I am determined to get even with them when I next see them, but you know, Selena, it's quite sinister and frightening."

Selina's story was just as dramatic, because she also was startled by someone jumping out of the shrubbery just beyond the pier, who took several photos of her running before disappearing into the wilderness. Next, two thugs were upon her and tried to molest her.

"So, Sam, I simply kicked them in the balls and left them howling in a heap on the sand, before two more kicks for good measure," Selina enthused, and the two of them collapsed with laughter.

"You know, Selina, I really need to pull myself together and stop my morose thoughts," said Sam. "Let's have some fun today, take a trip to the outlet stores across the causeway after breakfast. Easy for me, because I am free today, and you can forget your master's studies for a while and take a break."

"Sounds real cool. We could go to the neat open mall, have a browse at Victoria's Secret, and enjoy a really nice lunch at the Bistro."

Sam was starting to relax; the two youngsters chatted about their plans for the day, as they left the beach and strolled up the gentle incline towards the picnic tables. Just then, their hilarity abruptly stopped in midsentence, and they screamed in seeing a noose dangling from a stout branch of the old tree, with a bench placed underneath.

After their initial shock, Samantha exclaimed, "What on earth?"

Selina shouted, "Those evil bastards, Sammy; let's fight back and help the police identify them and bring them to justice."

"Yes, indeed, Selina. But there's more to it. My employers have the most amazing connections to crimefighters, and I am just about to call Rolf, who will know what to do."

Selina nodded and said, "Let's you and I stay here on this bench and be ready to provide any help to whoever comes to deal with this sorry matter."

In the meantime, back at the resort, Edward Pregowski arrived at Rolf and Sabine's apartment in order to follow up the puzzle of the peculiar delivery. He stroked his moustache, as he carefully looked at the three exhibits Rolf had spread on the round dining table.

"Wise move, guys, to keep these objects under wraps," the chief of police confirmed. "Dear Rolf and Sabine, you know of course that this is a serious attempt of intimidation. It's likely the first step of an aggressive campaign by the mysterious individual, who seems to have disappeared to Italy. Joyce Allan, our local chief of police, is on her way with a team of experts to analyse these sinister objects."

"Come on, Ed, let's have some coffee," Sabine suggested. "How about a toasted bacon sandwich whilst we wait?"

"Great idea, Sabine, and yes, bacon sandwich sounds perfect for me," Edward declared, just as Rolf's cell phone rang.

After a brief hello, he fired rapid and decisive instructions to the caller:

"Now, Sam, and your friend stay just where you are; don't draw

The Molehill

any attention to what you found. Act normal, and if need be, divert the attention of anyone who might approach. Chief Pregowski and I are on the way and will be there in five minutes."

"Come on, Ed, we need to drive to the picnic area, where our nanny, Samantha, discovered a noose hanging from an old tree near the leisure area."

Within minutes, the two men were on the approach to the building that flanked the picnic area, whilst Edward was on the phone to Chief Allan, who decided to meet the two young ladies at the picnic area.

As Rolf and Edward stepped out from their car, they saw the two young women sitting at one of the wooden tables, chatting, animatedly but with defiant looks on their faces.

"No one's been here, Rolf," Samantha confirmed, "but this is really weird, and it gave Selina and me the creeps."

"Don't worry, my dears, we'll get to the bottom of it," Edward reassured the youngsters. "And well done, for the way you handled the situation.

"Now let's have a quiet little chat; let me know any details of this morning's adventure, however trivial you think they are. Then anything unusual during the last few days you might have noticed, I would simply love to know." He looked at the two of them with an encouraging smile.

The young women looked at each other, then Samantha smiled and said, "We better tell you the full story. There were several incidents that concerned us since last weekend, so here goes." With a mischievous smile, she told her friend, "Why don't you start, Selina, because as a Princeton graduate, you are much brighter than me."

"Ok, you posh English cow, and just because you once owned the colonies, I guess I'll have to do what I'm told." Selina stuck her tongue out at Samantha.

As the two girls told their stories, Edward made copious notes, and Rolf kept a close watch, to divert any casual visitors, as he did not want them to see the object of their investigation. They soon heard a number of cars approaching, and then their location was invaded by several officers, led by their chief, Joyce Allan.

"Hi, Ed," the young woman called out. "Pleased to meet you, Mr

Brenner, so glad to see how well you are recovering from your accident almost two years ago."

"Thank you, Chief Allan, for all you did for my wife, when you arrived to break the news to her. Congratulations on your appointment as local chief of police."

"Thank you, sir, and now, let's get the show on the road. As you can see, my team have already taped off the scene, and they will concentrate on finding hand- and footprints on the benches, the table, and the tree. In the meantime, I see my good friend and mentor, Ed, is completing his interviews with the young ladies, just perfect for the two of us to review what he has gleaned. Thereafter, I am afraid I will have a more detailed conversation with each of them."

The efficiency of the experts was remarkable; they took photographs, collected samples, dusted for prints, and then carefully preserved evidence in special containers. Finally, the team declared the area open for business and departed in the direction of the causeway. Soon after, Rolf, Sabine, Edward, and Phyllis were relaxing in the living room of their apartment whilst their children were at poolside, with friends and their parents.

Sam and Selina were sunbathing on the lanai, sipping vodka and tonics, comparing notes about boyfriends, and indulging in general girl talk.

Selina took another sip of her cocktail, looked at Sam, and said, "You know, my funny friend, Mr Pregowski, and Chief Allan are absolutely right by advising us to stop running first thing in the morning or last thing at night; in any case, we should only visit the beach in pairs."

"That's a real pain, Selina. I love my early-morning and late-evening runs, but I guess it makes sense. We'll have to be ever such good girls and do what we're told."

"Now don't get carried away, Sam; let's just agree we will try to be ever such good girls within reason, as far as the beach is concerned, but other than that, such as boys, partying, and shopping, forget it."

"You cheeky little bitch, Selina, and yes, let's make a pact to be naughty and have fun except on the beach. I think that calls for a refill; cheers."

In Rolf and Sabine's apartment, they enjoyed a glass of wine with their close friends, Edward and Phyllis, a bubbly personality with headmistress of a private girls school written all over her. Her snow-white hair was coiffed in a series of plaits and a bun on top of her head, and she was generally known as a mini tornado.

"Now look, my dears," she declared and then a nonstop torrent followed: "first of all, I need another glass of wine, then the two gals will behave and stop running on their own early morning or late evening, and my Edward will keep his eye on them. Now, much more importantly, I have prepared six rib-eye steaks for the four of us, the two young ladies, and there are two special fresh burgers for the children ready to be put on the grill, so boys, off you go, fetch the meat from my kitchen, and get grilling down below. I shall fetch my giant bowl of salad, Sabine, and freshly baked cornbread."

As Rolf and Edward lit the new Webber barbecue, they enjoyed a beer, and Edward said, "You know, of course, that Joyce Allan has trebled surveillance on the beach with undercover cops, in addition to more frequent Coast Guard and police car patrols."

Rolf was pleased with how thorough the young police chief was handling the incident, and he told Edward about the mysterious delivery he had received at his HQ in England, just before leaving for the United States.

"Nigel Britton has taken the arrow, which appears to be from one of your original tribes in Colorado, to Fenella Hardwick; she is also analysing two photographs which worried us, one of the underground factory dungeon, where Belinda Carrington and Fiona Cameron, Professor Duncan Cameron's daughter, were held captive almost two years ago. And from the same period, a close-up of the Chicago factory blaze, which almost destroyed our business."

As the steaks and burgers sizzled away and a delicious aroma of char-grilled beef permeated the grounds, two speedboats were floating in the bay, observing the couples on the lanai through binoculars and a powerful telescope.

Chapter 15

Flight Encounters: North Atlantic

The flight to Denver took off on schedule, climbed steeply, momentarily dipped slightly in accordance with noise abatement regulations, and then soared higher; it made an elegant left turn and was now well on the way to Ireland. Soon the view of the Emerald Isle spread out below; looking down on the rugged countryside, Belinda Carrington's mind wandered back to the time when her endurance was stretched to the absolute limit, during the many weeks of her special forces training course in County Donegal.

It had all started with a gruelling selection process, shortly after she gained her commission at Sandhurst and joined the regiment. Her company commander decided she had all the necessary attributes to join a select group of specially equipped officers. Her natural courage, both physical and emotional strength, and resilience enabled her to withstand the rigors and occasionally simulated brutality of the course. She rejoined the regiment as a first lieutenant in the Intelligence Corps and further developed her skills in controlling complex operations, both at central command and in the field, where she excelled as a resourceful operator behind enemy lines and as an outstanding leader.

Belinda's current mission at MI5 was to work closely with Scotland Yard, the CIA, and the Swiss Secret Service; as one of the most promising young agents, she pursued specific lines of inquiry into the emerging threats to Rolf Brenner's operations in the UK, US, and Germany.

And now, she settled into her comfortable Club World seat and

The Molehill

looked forward to a well-deserved break. However, although she was on holiday, her natural curiosity and professional motivation had kicked in while waiting in the executive lounge prior to boarding. She had observed a trio of rather strange and colourful individuals, who spoke loudly in the unmistakable accent of the South of France, more specifically, the Camargue. Their vociferous and loud exchanges were at times intrusive, and the three men appeared to be oblivious of the fact that others, such as Belinda, spoke French.

The summary of the exchanges Belinda overheard amounted to general gripes about many different things, their suspicion of anything that was not French, and their plans for Colorado, which appeared to be related to their new employer, whom they had never met. They had been approached and recruited by a nasty woman who did not mince her words; she spoke with an unpleasant German accent and made it very clear that she was the boss. Horrible bitch, *"une vacherie,"* they agreed, but then, pouring more wine, they congratulated each other about the huge amount of money they were going to earn.

Belinda had already catalogued what she had learnt and resolved to keep her eyes and ears open in order to glean further information, as the flight proceeded towards the open Atlantic. She was also interested in Colonel Tarrant, with his clipped English accent, and his rugged companion, who spoke with a heavy northern German accent. She wondered how the two of them were connected; most of all, who was the colonel? Had she actually come across him somewhere in the past?

Her thoughts were interrupted by the cabin service director, who introduced himself with a cheerful, "Welcome on board, Miss Carrington. It's a real pleasure to meet you. I have been instructed to provide you with any assistance you require. Captain Chris Maynard knows you are on board and sends you his best wishes for an enjoyable flight."

"Thank you, Robert, how nice, and yes, in case I need some assistance, I will most certainly ask."

OK, guys, Belinda thought, *thanks for thinking of me. My bosses discreetly advised the captain and CSD about my identity. Who knows, I might wish to contact HQ, depending on what transpires during the next few hours.*

"May I present you with the menu and wine list, and perhaps offer you a glass of champagne?" suggested Stephen, who had specifically chosen the left-hand aisle of the aircraft in order to be able to serve the strikingly beautiful Miss Carrington.

"Thank you, and a nice glass of Sancerre would be perfect, whilst I study the menu," replied Belinda. After a while, she was served her beverage accompanied by warm South African macadamia nuts.

Belinda savoured her refreshing drink, was just about to recline and let her thoughts drift to the recent dramatic events, that had brought her here, for a time of relaxation, reflection, adjustment and then to focus with renewed energy on her career as one of the new generation of experts in fighting international crime. Her brief time of consideration was interrupted by a commotion a few seats ahead of her, where the three Frenchmen were seated in the middle row of the cabin, as Gaston Bleriot declared, how stupid the English were by not carrying his favourite drink, Pastis Ricard, on board!

Susan, the flight attendant who served the right-hand aisle of the aircraft handled the situation in perfect classical French and with a ravishing smile by recommending that the gentlemen might consider the fine French brands, that British Airways featured on their extensive wine and beverage list, including premium Champagne, fine wines, Grand Marnier, Cointreau, and a wonderful twenty-year-old Cognac. Bleriot grudgingly chose the latter; whilst Hubert chose the Bordeaux, and Luc opted for Champagne.

"May I please take your order for the meal, Miss Carrington," Stephen said. "May I recommend the sea bass as your main course?"

"Thank you, Stephen," replied Belinda. "That sounds fine, starting with the Evesham asparagus, please."

"Certainly, madam, and my colleague will offer appropriate wines in just a little while."

Almost an hour later, Belinda relaxed after her delicious meal, finished with British cheese and grapes, an indulgent dessert of traditional summer pudding, a small box of chocolates, and finally a small pot of chamomile tea. She was now ready to drift off and enjoy a relaxing snooze.

The Frenchman who was the most senior of the three acknowledged their lunch was surprisingly good; they had asparagus and smoked salmon starters, a choice of grilled fillet steak, sea bass, chicken with wild mushrooms, or pasta with pesto and grilled Mediterranean vegetables, followed by English cheeses, summer pudding, chocolates, and plenty of fine wine. They had obviously been prepared by a French chef.

As Susan cleared the dishes, she overheard these pronouncements and smiled; the trio of Frenchmen declined coffee and opted for more alcohol. Soon, however, all three of them had drifted off to sleep, with one of them, Hubert, starting to snore.

After about an hour, Belinda gradually came to after a light sleep; refreshed and invigorated, she asked for a cup of tea and started to take stock of the intriguing dynamics on board, including the three French passengers. Even more so the mysterious Colonel Tarrant and his German colleague; she decided to keep an eye on them and overhear their conversation, switching her attention to what they were planning to undertake in Colorado.

Unaware of the young woman's interest, a quiet debate was developing between the polished and stylish colonel and his rugged companion.

"Right, Albrecht, let's just recap," Tarrant whispered. "You were recruited by our section chief, Hannah Gerber, and considered suitable for the initial task you were instructed to complete. Miss Gerber recommended you to our ultimate Lord and master, who scrutinized your background in the greatest of details and then approved your appointment."

Belinda moved to a vacant window seat on the left-hand side of the aircraft, in order to admire the view of the dark blue Atlantic and the occasional ocean liner on its way towards an unknown destination. But in reality, this brought her within earshot of the two passengers; she observed their interaction and animated body language.

"So what have you got to say for yourself, Gerhard Albrecht?" Tarrant hissed.

"Colonel Tarrant, sir, I was so proud of being recruited by your powerful organization; I want to prove how much I can achieve."

"Well, Albrecht, you cocked up big time," whispered Tarrant. "What on earth possessed you to leave the mountain and to let the five targets escape? Not only that, you spoke disrespectfully to Miss Gerber, who had to give you a serious talking to and your first verbal warning."

Tarrant had left his seat and was leaning against the bulkhead that faced their two seats. He towered over the hapless German, looking intimidating, and hissed, "Come on, now, you have ten minutes to make your presentation; before we land in Denver, I want to know how you intend to complete the task I briefed you about last night."

With this, he disappeared through the curtain, walked into the galley, poured a glass of red wine and then chose from a selection of savoury snacks that were displayed for passengers to help themselves.

The elegant young lady appeared next to him, helping herself to a plate of cut fruit, some biscuits, and a sparkling mineral water. He was tempted to start a conversation, but something about this passenger worried him. Her gaze made him feel unusually insecure. He tried to recall if she was a celebrity, or might he have come across her at some time in the past?

No time for diversions, he decided; he nodded to the statuesque lady with a smile and disappeared between the curtains that led back to his seat.

He glowered at the young man and told him to outline his plan. "Now, Albrecht, lower your voice and make sure no one can see any of these documents."

Albrecht and Tarrant continued their conversation at low key, but Belinda had inserted a miniature receiver into her earphones; she seemed to be nodding to her favourite tunes, but in reality was listening to every single word the two of them exchanged.

As she strolled down the aisle on the way to the galley area, the perceptive young woman glanced at the two men who were engrossed in a debate and to spot further details, including several A4-size pages with clear headings, and larger documents showing maps and blueprints of buildings. There was a third type of paper, which was of particular concern, as it seemed to illustrate a detailed electronic device, linked to a timing mechanism, that could actually be an explosive device.

There was no doubt the pair of them warranted further investigation; Belinda decided to include the three French business travellers in her

The Molehill

message to HQ. Just then, their raised voices, in French of course, fuelled by copious measures of alcoholic beverages, started to disturb some of the other passengers.

"Hubert, you idiot, you could not possibly do that without being detected," shouted Gaston, "and Luc, you are an imbecile to encourage him to embark on such a risky project."

"But Gaston, we must take risks to be successful," Luc replied. "We must be formidable, courageous, and totally ruthless; that's the only way we can impress Miss Horrible."

Hubert started to sing a little song about the horrible cow who said she was their boss.

Shaun, a tall, muscular steward, appeared in the aisle behind the three passengers, who were now becoming somewhat of a nuisance. His loud and deep voice boomed, "Yes, gentlemen, may I be of assistance?"

The men were unsure what to say; Shaun switched into perfect French and recommended a cup of tea or a nice strong coffee to accompany the sandwiches, scones, and cakes that would be served shortly. Shaun also added a polite request for the gentlemen to please lower their voices.

Belinda smiled at how admirably the cabin crew had calmed a potentially explosive situation. And thinking about explosives, she thought, *Yes, I now have sufficient detail to alert the head office.* She asked to see Robert, who escorted her to the flight deck. Captain Maynard was well aware of Belinda's reputation as a foremost agent in the fight against international crime. He welcomed her with an offer of any assistance she required.

Soon afterwards, Brad Coulter, a senior agent of the organization in the United States, was alerted and planned the deployment of his troupe in response to a detailed conversation with HQ in London. His agents would be in position at Denver's airport, prepared to conduct surveillance of the three French businessmen arriving on BA 0219. A separate team would focus on Colonel Tarrant and Gerhard Albrecht. Brad would oversee both operations and communicate regularly with London.

Belinda was relaxing in her Club World seat, smiling; her restful flight to Denver had developed into an exciting adventure. But now it was time for her to switch into holiday mode and look forward to relaxation, reflection, and physically demanding adventures in the Rocky Mountains. It was time to recharge her batteries. As BA 0219 began its final approach and landed on time; it was an excellent flight; Belinda was unaware of the dangers she would face and the dramatic developments that would tax her endurance and resourcefulness to the limit.

Chapter 16

Conspiracy: Switzerland and Italy

As the aircraft banked, Pia Marinello, cabin services director, was delighted to see the delta of the River Po in northern Italy below; the jet then headed towards the Dolomites and behind that the Alps before the final stage of the flight to Zurich's airport.

After taking off from Johannesburg, the eight passengers in first class enjoyed a pleasant flight, enhanced by delicious meals, refreshing beverages, and plenty of opportunities to relax. Some enjoyed the latest movies and popular programmes, while others listened to the news, music, or podcasts.

Pia was pleased to see the Italian landscape below because of her imminent holiday in Bologna, which her cousin, Maya von Gunten, had so highly recommended. Maya, who looked after Pia's apartment during her frequent absences abroad, had volunteered to remind Pia's manager she was going on holiday; she even made all the necessary arrangements for hotel bookings, transport, and one particularly exciting stay for three days at an old monastery.

As the flight progressed, Pia was pleased to watch her crew's impeccable service; they offered fresh fruit, tiny hot ham croissants, wafer-thin alpine cheese, air-dried beef, and small slices of smoked bacon, accompanied by fresh rye bread, perfectly brewed coffee, tea, and freshly squeezed orange juice, in addition to champagne and fine Swiss wines.

The snow-covered peaks of the Alps were soon left behind, revealing lakes, villages, towns, and the Jura Mountains to the left, before a smooth and perfect landing at Zurich Airport. Pia complimented her crew, including those who had served business and economy class, and everyone wished her a lovely holiday. After completing her administrative formalities and a brief chat with her manager, she strode briskly to the car park, got into her red open-top sports car, blasting her favourite tunes.

A few days later, Maya von Gunten carefully entered Pia's apartment while Anton and the concierge were distracted by a delivery of furniture. She used the service stairs and went into the apartment, where she put her carefully constructed plan into action, starting with a perfect indulgence of a luxurious bath, listening to her favourite radio station and sipping a glass of pink Champagne. A few hours' sleep then helped her to relax, unwind, and prepare her thoughts for the next phase, which was to pack her suitcase, her rollaway, and her hand luggage.

She then went into the service stairs and snuck into the attic, where Pia's personal storage area was, and retrieved a container hidden behind suitcases, boxes, blankets, and linen. She brought the compact container back to the apartment and secured it under the false bottom of her suitcase, covering it by her combat clothes and boots.

She placed the packed cases, rollaway, and hand luggage in the hall and then kitted herself out in the smart uniform of a Swissair cabin service director. She completed her preparations with Pia's makeup and included more of this in her hand luggage, alongside Pia's special pass, paperwork, and schedule of operations.

Right, Pia, she thought, as she entered the elevator and stepped into the lobby, where Anton looked up, beamed, and enthused, "Miss Marinello, welcome back. I thought you were on holiday for another ten days; it's such a pleasure to see you. Your car is still being serviced but will be ready for you after your return. In the meantime, I have a taxi on standby if you need transport."

"Thank you, Anton. I will pick up something really nice for you in Miami."

"You're welcome, Miss Marinello. Do you have any special wishes for your return?"

"No, Anton, I left all my instructions for Miss von Gunten, and I know you will look after her, as always."

The Molehill

"Um," Anton grunted as he thought of Maya's sharp little quips, not at all like the lovely Miss Marinello's kind comments.

Later that afternoon, as Maya joined the hubbub of the crew reporting to board the aircraft, she felt at ease. She happily chatted with the crew, many of whom she had met with Pia at social events, and she was delighted with their reaction to her being in charge.

Maya had studied Pia's personal manuals and textbooks, and read all the coursework which had propelled Pia to her senior position. She felt confident in taking charge of her lively crew. She had also studied Pia's approach to colleagues, to both cabin and flight deck crew, and to the passengers. Although she felt that her cousin was too soft and easy in dealing with customers, she adapted Pia's style.

The flight was ready for departure; Maya smirked at the thought of her cousin in Bologna, where her new leaders had organised a very special experience for the unsuspecting stewardess.

Whilst Maya was flying to Miami, developments in the north of Italy also took shape; two helicopters approached a meadow near Bologna's Santa Lucia Monastery. They landed just a few yards in front of the main portal, where Hannah Gerber, Brother Anselmo, and three of his monks stood to attention.

The doors of the helicopters opened; Musgrove stepped down and prepared the way for Milton Adams, who descended and barked out orders: "Gerber, breakfast, then the board meeting; get the show on the road."

Hannah, dressed in combat fatigues and wearing a black beret, saluted and barked her instructions at Anselmo and his team.

Breakfast took place in the underground veranda, lit up by artificial sunshine and enhanced by masses of foliage, plants, and flowers, almost as if it were out in the open. The lavish Italian breakfast included melon, Parma ham, provolone cheese, soft mountain cheeses, rustic bread, sliced sausages, scrambled eggs with white shaved truffle, panettone, and plenty of grapes from the nearby vineyards.

The boardroom had been carefully prepared by Brother Anselmo, and as the team assembled, Milton looked pleased. He opened the meeting by saying, "Your preliminary reports appear to be satisfactory, but now it's time for chapter and verse, with nothing more than perfection acceptable to me. Woe betide any of you if you fail to present me with progress during the last two weeks and precise plans for the rest of the month."

Musgrove rose and outlined the agenda, then invited Brother Anselmo to present the monastery's state of play.

"Blessings to all of you," the monk intoned. "As you will see, ladies and gentlemen, the private suites for all our guests are quite superb. I hope you will enjoy the many aspects of our hospitality."

"Come on, Monk, cut the domestic crap," Milton snapped. "What I want is a detailed update of your operational readiness to explode into action."

"Master, I am pleased to report all special facilities according to your personal taste and instructions are available in the second level of the basement near the internal waterfall; all the preparations have been made to welcome your secret guest."

Milton grinned and said, "Full marks, Monk. I look forward to my entertainment, but now Musgrove, you are in the spotlight, so give us the lowdown."

"Master, my secret agent in Switzerland, who tipped us off about the planned raid, has infiltrated another organisation. A special guest will join us shortly in this location.

"In addition, I have supervised threats to Rolf Brenner Associates, their subsidiaries in the United States, their lawyer, financial leaders, and RB's personal family and staff. These are starting to destabilise the individuals and their organisations."

"OK, Musgrove, but be assured I demand proof of these details. I want to see you at two o'clock sharp, so shut up, you ugly little dwarf, and let Gerber continue."

Hannah Gerber moved to the centre of the table, saluted, and presented the progress made by her agents in the United States: the Cockney Demons, Huntingdon and Petroni, Albrecht, and Colonel Tarrant. They were now ready to spring into action and deliver his objectives.

"All this promising twaddle does not mean a thing unless it starts to produce my results," Milton snapped. "I want the three of you to prepare for a tough and uncomprehensive personal debriefing with me this afternoon. So look out and be scared, very, very scared."

Chapter 17

Boulder, Colorado

Arlene Wilson felt cross today and was in a bad mood although she was obliged to smile and to make her customers feel special as she served breakfast on this sunny Friday morning at Reno's Restaurant just off the upper end of Pearl Street on the outskirts of the city of Boulder in Colorado. Her bad mood was in contrast to this warm and sunny day, where business was brisk and Arlene's share of the tips looked promising, to say the least.

What it boiled down to was she intensely disliked having to serve people and quite frankly felt this should be the other way around. She had vowed this serving customer drudgery would indeed be reversed at some stage in the not-too-distant future. Yes, her carefully crafted plans would become reality, and she would surprise them all and show them who was boss.

She was tall, slim, even statuesque, and quite attractive when she smiled, which was not very often on this particular day, and even when she attempted to do so her expression remained hard, and her pale blue eyes looked cold as ice. Now in her early thirties, she still had long blonde hair tied in a ponytail which swished defiantly, touching the top of her shoulder blades as she strode up the few steps and along the upper level to collect more food for another table of customers.

Her face would have been almost beautiful had it not been for a slightly masculine trait which was accentuated by her stern demeanour on this particular Friday morning. As she emerged again carrying one of those large trays of dishes, her body looked tight, much too tight, but as she served the meals and the three young men engaged her in some friendly banter, she visibly relaxed and responded with a forced smile but gracefully swung her hips as she disappeared through one of the service doors.

"Hi, beautiful, let me have your cash printout as soon as you can," the duty manager called after Arlene as she passed him on the way to the cash point. He was stunned by her reaction, which consisted of a sharp "What?" and a vicious glare. She then slammed the door in his face as she stormed out of sight and into the kitchen beyond. The sound of a further commotion and a heated debate could then be heard.

She fumed as she let off steam to her friend Lesley, the head chef, and burst into a torrent of abuse about this jerk of a manager, the indignity of having to serve stupid people, and what the hell was the kitchen doing by making her wait for the next batch of food.

The young chef smiled, put a comforting arm around Arlene's shoulder, and said, "Come on, darling Arly, let me give you a Lesley hug."

She managed to calm her friend down after a while. Encouraged, Arlene slowly regained her composure and was able to resume her duties in a moderately satisfactory way, although both her facial expression and body language remained challenging for the rest of the morning shift.

This was until she was finally able to change into what she called civilized clothes, to walk round the corner, jump into her car, and roar down Corona Trail towards her apartment in the leafy northern suburbs of Boulder. As she drove her iridescent blue Saab convertible along the avenue, with her ponytail flowing in the wind, few people would have suspected she had spent her morning as a waitress in a popular restaurant to supplement her meagre basic wages with tips that rarely exceeded 10 percent these days. Observers would have been even more surprised by the luxurious apartment she called her own.

That impression would be further accentuated by her reappearance an hour later, clad in the most exquisitely tailored linen suit, Carvela shoes, matching gloves, designer accessories, and sunglasses that complimented her elegant appearance. Her hair was now piled up on top of her head in a stylish French pleat, and she looked truly exceptional as she stepped into her car and took off for Denver.

Her day had started well enough this morning with a telephone call from Gino, her live-in partner, who was already well on his way along the picturesque road leading from the Eisenhower Johnson Memorial Tunnel, driving one of the recognizably branded O'Reilly Inc trucks, delivering a load of goods to one of the company's major customers in San Francisco. He had been confident and cheerful as ever, and as a result, Arlene felt comfortable and happy.

As she accelerated, her smooth radio tunes were interrupted by a telephone call, and when she answered, she was amused to hear what she was sure was an Italian accent who said, *"Buon giorno, signora* Arlena, this is a Brother Anselmo from the Santa Lucia Monastery in Bologna with a message for you."

There followed a brief conversation, and after hanging up, Arlene nodded, smiled, and shrieked with joy; she was in a buoyant mood and on her way to start a new adventure.

BA 0219 was nearing Denver after a long, pleasant flight from Heathrow. The cabin services director confirmed that Belinda's driver was ready and waiting at the VIP arrivals lounge and suggested a glass of pink Champagne before arrival, which Belinda thoroughly enjoyed, with a few Tuille biscuits. Captain Maynard joined Belinda for a brief chat and presented her with a special printout of a secret message from MI5.

As the aircraft banked to the left, the Flatiron Range and the peaks of the Rocky Mountains beyond appeared. Belinda marvelled at the majesty of the view and smiled as she overheard Gaston, who seemed to be the senior and certainly was the loudest French passenger, acknowledging that "yes, the American mountains are quite nice, but do not compare with Mont Blanc, which is the tallest and most beautiful mountain in the whole of the world, yes, that's absolutely right."

Belinda had always loved the approach to Denver, especially the distant view of the airport, which was designed to look like a village of tepees. The aircraft cruised the last few miles and gently descended for the final approach and a smooth landing on runway 3A.

The captain and cabin crew beamed and said farewell to the passengers;

The Molehill

on leaving the aircraft, Belinda was delighted to spot a British Airways special services agent, ready to escort her to the VIP arrivals lounge. She always enjoyed the stroll towards the exit at Denver, enhanced by wonderful sounds of native drums and local Indian chanting. In addition, there were superb paintings, photographs, and pictures of Sitting Bull, Buffalo Bill, and their families to admire on the way.

As she approached the main entrance, she noticed a tall, statuesque woman whose regal bearing clearly captivated those around her. Her designer dress was styled like a North American Indian shift. She wore her black hair in a stylish knot at the nape of her neck, which accentuated her classical features, high cheekbones, dark almond-shaped eyes, and expressive eyebrows. She wore no makeup; it was not needed on account of her beautiful skin tone, which suggested the possibility of a partial and distant ancestry, related to the original inhabitants of the United States.

Belinda's eyes briefly met those of the mysterious woman, and there seemed to be a slight flicker of recognition from the lady, but not long enough for Belinda to make contact. This was because of the sudden arrival of a smart young woman, who introduced herself and then escorted the beautiful stranger to the exit. Belinda looked outside and saw her get into an iridescent blue sports car.

Belinda took a photo of the car and made a note of the registration number. She briefly called head office to report her latest observations leading up to her arrival and also to say how much she appreciated their arrangement of a security guard to drive her to Boulder instead of her original plan of renting a 4x4. She then followed the BA customer services agent to the executive arrivals suite, where a refreshing shower was followed by a delicious brunch.

Her driver then escorted her to a limousine, with all her luggage safely stowed for her journey to Boulder. Belinda relaxed and enjoyed their progress through the picturesque countryside on the way to her hotel; she reflected about her encounter in the arrivals hall at the airport. She was quite certain now that she had met the beautiful lady in the past, or at least heard about her from one of her associates.

Soon the outskirts of Boulder's attractive, leafy suburbs came into view, then the lively town centre before the attractive parkway towards the mountains and her destination, the university's hotel. Belinda's team had originally booked her into the exclusive St. Julien Hotel and Spa, but she preferred to soak up the atmosphere of the beautiful grounds of the university, to meet the faculty, have a chat with the students, and see Ralfie, the famous buffalo and the university's mascot, in his compound.

When they reached their destination, Belinda was surprised to be greeted by Professor Cameron resplendent in his kilt, his daughter Fiona, the dean of the college, Sir Lewis Pickford in his regalia, and two senior students.

"Welcome to Boulder University, Commander Carrington," said the dean. "You know Professor Cameron and his daughter Fiona, of course, and these are my senior students, Jabar and Dyani."

"Thank you for this lovely welcome, Your Honour, and what a delight to meet courageous Jabar and the lovely fallow deer, Dyani."

The two youngsters beamed, and Dyani triumphantly said, "See Jabar, I told you that Miss Carrington's background was similar to ours, and Commander, it is such an honour to make your acquaintance. We simply can't wait for your lecture tomorrow."

"Yes, it's simply lovely to be home in every possible sense," said Belinda, as the group moved to the lobby to arrange an escort to her suite.

At about the same time, Fenella Hardwick arrived at her luxurious suite at the St Julian Hotel and Spa after taking her leave from the animated, lively Arlene, who had met her at Denver International and then drove her to Boulder, happily chatting to her until they reached the hotel. A very attractive young woman, Fenella thought, but somehow, there were somethings hidden, a hint of a mysterious background, which her experienced lawyers mind identified.

And how right Fenella was, as Arlene screeched around the corner and roared down the lovely leafy parkway on her way home. "Yess, yess, yess," she shrieked, "not long to go now for my elevation to serve the master. That silly Italian bouffon said so when he interrupted my drive from Boulder. Yes, I will prepare the electronic device and accurately plant it for a big bang."

After settling into her luxurious suite, Fenella called Lord Britton, who was in a buoyant mood, full of enthusiasm and outstanding news about the breakthrough he had achieved on Wall Street and in connection with an impressive number of his personal business contacts.

"Fenella, this is what's going to happen now: We will take the battle directly to the opposition with their current bases in New York, Colorado, Italy, and Switzerland. But for now, I wish you a few wonderful days in your original home country. I will be in touch with regular updates and join you in Boulder very soon."

Chapter 18

Retribution: Southwest Florida

One misty autumnal morning, Samantha powered along the beach as part of her morning run, savouring the pleasure of solitude, the sound of the sea gently lapping against the shore, and the call of the many birds that populated this part of the island.

Sam had set off early at 06.30, quite simply because she wanted to be on her own for a while, to keep her fitness levels in top shape, and to rejoice about her good fortune; she enjoyed a lively job as nanny, teacher, and manager of her employer's household back at their lovely home in England.

Soon the young woman was joined by early residents, who appeared from the walkways and paths through shrubbery from local resorts, some of them jogging along the beach, others practicing the Sanibel Stoop by bending over and searching the superb collection of shells which had accumulated during the night. The joyful sound of children chasing each other and the peaceful scene of older visitors wandering along the shore and admiring the dolphins which occasionally appeared made her smile.

"Ok, Sammy, time to turn up the tempo," the young athlete said to herself as she increased her pace for a short spurt to the pier, where she stopped for a while to chat to the fishermen who were hauling in their catch from the depths of the sea below.

"Bye, guys," Sam called. "Good luck, and enjoy a lovely day."

She accelerated along the beach. At the inlet which led up to the rest area with the tables, benches, and the notorious tree, she noticed the police tapes had been removed. Chief Joyce Allan's forensic and investigative teams were now undoubtedly refining their research of the evidence, hoping to identify who had caused such an unpleasant incident with a dangling noose, taking photographs of the ladies, and accosting Sam and her friends on the beach.

Investigations appear to be in hand, Samantha thought. *But Chief Allen's resources are obviously stretched; will they be able to find the hoodlums? Geeze, a frightening thought: they might slip through the net and chase us down the beach with a noose.*

She accelerated with renewed enthusiasm around the large bend and thought, *Scaredy cat may be, but my worries are as dark as these storm clouds which are now gathering to the east, so for f...s sake let's get out of here.* This was where the dolphins could normally be seen. She increased her pace along the long home-straight to the resort.

"Well, good morning, my Lady Samantha," a cheerful voice called as Sam's tall and statuesque friend overtook her; she elegantly pirouetted and then curtsied in front of her.

"Arise, Lady Commander Selina, and aw come on and give me a hug, you crazy colonial mare."

The two of them embraced, burst into laughter, and walked hand in hand towards the resort's swimming pool.

They were joyfully greeted by those residents already relaxing on the sun loungers or seated at the round tables.

Then "Hi guys," chirped a cheerful voice from the middle of the pool. "Now are you coming to join me, so I can show you how we smash swimming records back home?"

"Aw, g'day, g'day to you, Waltzing Matilda," sang the two of them with gusto.

"And say, Victoria, shouldn't you be in bed," Samantha added, "seeing that it's midnight in Melbourne right now?"

"Good on you, mate, our lovely sophisticated Lady Samantha and eminent Princetown Commander Selina," Victoria replied. "So glad to see the two of you, because I have crucial information and a plan for the three of us to discuss, so my unit 1C in half an hour, please."

"Sure thing, bossy boots Aussi Victoria, see you at nine thirty."

As Sam mounted the steps to her apartment, she reflected on some of the recent dramas and wondered how she might best support Rolf, Sabine, and their business. The dark clouds of an approaching storm, which was expected to make landfall by late evening, were not the only shadow to make Sam think about the recent threats, intimidation, and innuendos about Rolf and Sabine, their family, and their business. All this in addition to harassment on the beach, assault, and suggestive threats, not to mention a dangling noose. Finally, a mysterious yacht, observing Rolf's family, their nanny, and her friends with special binoculars and cameras.

Chief Joyce Allan had deployed her team, and they were now hunting the two culprits and also the hooligans on their motorbikes, who had threatened the family in Naples. Such a large area to cover, and Samantha wondered if she and her friends could help the police to flush out the culprits.

The trio were soon sitting on Victoria's lanai, chatting, comparing notes, and enjoying a morning cocktail with a most delicious array of delicacies Victoria had conjured up.

After a while, the statuesque Australian girl sounded her spoon against a glass and announced, "Guys, I would like you to join me on the war path to fight and eliminate these unsavoury elements which have been such a threat; they're really scary and a continuous cause of annoyance.

"But first of all, I have some crucial news which my uncle, who is the Australian ambassador to the United States, confirmed to me this morning: Last night, there were arrests in the Bronx and in lower Manhattan, rounding up some members of the Cockney Demons. Lieutenant Simmons's hit squad, led by sergeants Ray Kenny in Manhattan and Lara Pregowski in the Bronx, found their locations and arrested a few of them; however, the majority managed to escape, as they were holed up in a third location."

"Aw," exclaimed Selina, "may be good news in a small way, but absolute crap overall."

"It seems the majority of them are still at large," Victoria said, "and who knows what scary plans they are hatching right now?"

"Absolutely," said Sam. "Two years ago, they set fire to Rolf and Sabine's factory in Chicago, and a few days ago, they murdered an old couple and their staff, who had planned major investments and promotions for Rolf Brenner Inc."

"Yep," Selina said. "Let us wish Simmons and his NYPD team every success to track down the rest of them and also those who planted the lethal bomb in Queens."

"Right, girls, we are where we are," announced Victoria, "so now we need to help Chief Allan to find the nasty band of motorcyclists threatening beach runners. Therefore, I'd like to make a call to arms, so let's pick up our swords, gird our loins, and plan a dynamic approach."

There was spontaneous applause and loud cheers from the three of them, as well as raucous laughter about their girded loins.

Once the three of them calmed down, they began discussing the details of a possible operation; Selina Nelson would lead the campaign. Their first task was to scrutinize the popular shopping areas where the marauding gangs had been seen. Victoria was to cover the popular stores and adjacent areas north of Highway 41; Samantha would take care of Fort Myers Beach, the Health Park, and the nearby supermarkets, whilst Selina would go to Edison Mall, downtown Fort Myers, and the surrounding areas.

In the evening, the three young women met after enthusiastically walking miles, observing, noting down details, and taking photographs; they went to Selina's unit and consolidated their findings, after plenty of refreshments: grilled steaks, eggs, salad, fruit, cheese, and ice cream.

The result was a dossier of sightings, but far more importantly, some of the secret locations had been pinpointed as possible hiding places. As the three of them enjoyed a celebratory drink on the lanai, they noticed a small yacht with the tell-tale lights of night binoculars and cameras in action offshore.

Just then, three police speedboats roared up and converged on the yacht; they surrounded and boarded the boat, then took it in tow, disappearing round the lighthouse corner to cheers and applause by the three young ladies.

"Well, guys," Samantha said, "I was tempted to suggest we make some rude signs for those idiots on board, but when I popped to the kitchen a while ago, I called Chief Allan and reported them. She obviously had anticipated it and prepared for a raid."

"You cheeky mare," said Victoria, "but how very, very clever. Let's toast all of us and Chief Allan's team with a mega cheer and a few more glasses of Californian chardonnay.'

The following morning, Selina contacted Chief Allan to outline their activities and see if they could help identify the subversive individuals on the beach, the bikers, and whoever placed the noose at the picnic area. The young police chief was intrigued by the possibilities Selina outlined and asked the three of them to meeting with her at their earliest opportunity.

Updating Chief Allan and her senior team was a lively, positive session; the young ladies presented their findings and explanations, which proved to be a valuable guide to rounding up and arresting the individuals Selina, Samantha, and Victoria had managed to identify. Chief Allan said the detailed information would pave the way for her detectives to round up the gang and clear out southwest Florida's threat from those particular criminals.

Two weeks later, the miscreants were behind bars, and the initiative by the trio of young women was acknowledged by the commissioner of police, the mayor, and the directors of the resort as an example of international collaboration.

Chapter 19

The Monastery: Switzerland and Italy

One misty autumnal morning in the historical Swiss town of Baden, the start of the day was announced at 06.15, as always, by the bells of the wonderful old Catholic church, which is situated in the *Kirchplatz*, the main square.

Not far away, on the top floor of a luxurious building, which combines business locations on the lower floors and private apartments above, a favourite radio station started with a cheerful tune at exactly the same time as the wake-up call of the melodious church bells. Young Pia Marinello, however, was already fully dressed and happily singing to the tune whilst putting on the last touches of her makeup.

"Hudihuy," she cheered, celebrating her freedom without a duty flight today; instead, she was taking a leisurely journey in business class to Italy for a welcome break from her busy life. She also looked forward to the special treat her cousin Maya had organised for her to spend a few days in an old monastery on the hills above the town of Bologna.

Pia got ready to go and left a few notes for Maya, who looked after her home during the young woman's regular absence; she took a final glance at her image in the full-length mirror, adjusted her Ellesse jacket, picked up her Radley bag, took her red Victorinox rollaway, and got the lift to the reception area.

"Aw, Miss Marinello, you look absolutely stunning and ready for your vacation," Anton the rotund porter enthused, as Pia stepped into the reception hall.

"Thank you, dear Anton. Tell me, are we ready for me to catch my flight?"

"Most certainly, madam; your car has been washed and polished, the interior is absolutely perfect, with a light spray of your favourite fragrance."

"Sounds wonderful, Concierge; Miss von Gunten's instructions are ready for her in my apartment, and please remind her of the date when I shall return."

Anton blushed and wiped a tear from his eye. *She actually called me dear and concierge*, he thought with a sigh.

A few minutes later, Pia's red sports car sprung into life as she drove out of the underground car park and soon accelerated on the road to Zurich Airport. Traffic was quite light at this time of the day, and she reached the parking area in no time. The young woman nodded to the security guard at the airport's business area and parked in her personal allocated space.

The airport concourse was buzzing as always, and although Pia was tempted to explore the many retail outlets, she decided to check in for her flight and then to pop along the executive lounge, where she could have a light breakfast before boarding the aircraft.

"*Bella,* Pia *mia,*" beamed her manager as she walked up to his desk.

"And a very good and brilliant morning to you, Beat; guess what? Knowing how awfully you will miss my sparkling personality during my absence, I could not possibly leave without saying, 'Arrivederci capo Beato.'" She giggled.

"Come on, behave," her boss said, chuckling. "Lovely Pialina, I just have to say, that your last report of the flight from Johannesburg was absolutely spot on. In fact, our GM was so impressed that he instructed building services to implement your recommendations in the departure lounge at Joey airport."

"Heya, Pia darling, what a surprise," a smiling young flight attendant chirped, "and there were all of us thinking, that last evening, we had spotted you boarding the flight to Miami."

"Not me, our lovely, cheerful Ursi, as I am off to bella Italia for a short holiday, arranged by my cousin Maya."

Ursula Kammerer looked puzzled for a while but cheerfully responded by wishing Pia a lovely break, plenty of panettone, and the adulation of the handsome Italian boys.

"Cheers, Ursi and Beat; time for me to spoil myself in the executive departure lounge," Pia called, waving to her friends, and then she was on her way to Bologna.

In the meantime, 240 miles south from Zurich Airport, a glorious morning dawned on the peaceful hillside above Bologna. The natural sounds of birds, insects, and the tinkling of a herd of goats' bells added to the peace and quiet of this rustic environment.

Just then, the sound of the Santa Lucia Monastery bells were joined by the powerful bells of the many different churches and a cathedral in the picturesque town of Bologna further down, at the foot of the hillside.

"Time for matins, Brothers," announced Anselmo, as the monks gathered and followed him in line to their place of worship.

Brother Anselmo was in a buoyant mood about how he had taken control of the monastery, the building, and as almoner, all financial and operational aspects of Santa Lucia. He was now in effect the leader, because old Abbot Mario Machinello was ailing and hardly aware of anything but the privacy of his personal cell.

Anselmo was called *Cormaccia*, the Black Crow by the local population of the town because of his beaky nose and the way he flapped his black habit when he flamboyantly walked through the town. He was well known and highly respected, but people were also suspicious of his ruthless ways of achieving success.

His pride and joy was the design and construction of the secret passages underneath the old monastery; he presented it to the master's section chiefs on schedule, thanks to unlimited funds. All the work was completed in secrecy, and the contractors involved mysteriously disappeared, never to be seen again.

As the building slowly sprung into life with the sound of religious services and domestic duties, Musgrove, Milton Adam's chief of staff, as always dressed in a formal morning suit, surveyed proceedings and the preparation of a lavish breakfast for Milton and his senior section chiefs, which was due to be followed by an intensive review of the master plan.

The plan's purpose was to discredit Rolf Brenner's organizations; intimidate his family, business associates, suppliers, and clients; and most of all create doubts about their business and manipulate the media to drastically decrease the value of the shares, All this in preparation for Adams to swoop in and acquire these successful businesses and incorporate them into his massive empire.

Milton's new headquarters was invisible underneath the monastery, lavishly appointed and constructed in such a way that both windows and glass ceilings gave the impression of being in a park full of trees, shrubs, lawns, flowers, and wildlife.

The breakfast selection was equally enticing, including a plethora of Italian and international specialties, refreshing beverages, and sparkling champagne. Musgrove, Hannah Gerber, chief of Europe, Colonel Tarrant, chief of operations, Christopher Huntingdon, chief of USA, and Brother Anselmo were waiting for Milton Adams's arrival. The five of them scrutinized each other, wondering what achievements they would present or, far worse, what failures they had to explain.

When the door swung open, all five of them shot up and stood to attention, except Anselmo who crossed himself and said, "God be with us."

Milton marched in, glared at the five of them, and took his seat at the head of the table.

"Right, Musgrove, chapter and verse, pronto," bellowed Adams.

"Your eminence, I suggest the order of the presentations will start with Brother Anselmo, who has completed all the building work and related facilities on time and within budget, including these secret palatial facilities."

"Clever monk, Cormaccia, but I'll be watching you. Now clear off," Milton snapped.

Anselmo, looking peeved, swung his black habit and disappeared behind the leather security door.

Hannah Gerber, in military combat gear and wearing a black beret, stood, saluted, and spoke in her crisp, precise English with a hint of

The Molehill

German. "Sir, we have successfully undermined Rolf Brenner, his family, and their nanny by subtle and threatening activities which have unnerved them to such an extent they have sought refuge in their apartment in southwest Florida."

"What?" Adams yelled. "I have never heard of such an amateurish childish campaign. The Brenners were not intimidated but were galvanized into securing a formidable team of crime prevention experts and lawyers, who are now plotting our downfall. So shut up, Gerber, and your other failure near Hamburg is equally as embarrassing."

"Yes, sir, I know, and after eliminating those guilty of failure in Florida, I enlisted Colonel Tarrant's help in knocking the German agent into shape in Colorado. I'd like to point out our dramatic success in Switzerland, where I recruited a mole who helped us avoid an attack by the Swiss Secret Service. This particular operator is exceptional, shrewd, ruthless, lethal with the crossbow, and currently on the way for our final showdown in Colorado."

"Two failures, one success, and some developments which had better be spectacular, so no promotion, Gerber, and only the ultimate success will determine your fate, so Commando Girl, bloody well watch it."

Huntingdon then stood up and was met by a barrage of abuse from Adams.

"Huntingdon, you and Elna Patroni have cocked up big time; you failed to eliminate those leaders, judges, and crime fighters. Instead, you killed innocent employees and guests at Cuccione's restaurant."

"Furthermore, many of the Manhattan-based Cockney Demons were eliminated by Lieutenant Simmons and his team. Your childish campaign with paintings and drawings to intimidate those in power are just a joke. I want you to leave this room and go outside, where Anselmo is waiting to deal with you." A crestfallen Huntingdon meekly left the room, never to be seen again.

Adams then shouted, "Musgrove, your briefing about all these failures put me firmly in the picture. I want you to continue, but don't cock it up, you ugly little toad.

"Tarrant, I am putting you in charge of the United States with immediate effect; Gerber will be your number one, and having closed down all the hair-brained schemes in England, southwest Florida, and New York, you will now focus on Colorado, whilst I remain in Bologna for the time being. First task, Tarrant, eliminate Patroni and Musgrove; throw Huntingdon into the underground lake. Then provide me with my special entertainment; I need a break after sorting out this bloody mess."

A few miles south of the monastery, Pia Marinello was enjoying a glass of local Valpolicella and a tasty selection of salami, Bel Paese, and Gorgonzola cheeses with fresh grapes, figs, and pine nuts.

She sat on the raised terrace overlooking the Piazza Maggiore and took great delight in watching the colourful activity right in front of her. Old and young enjoyed the late afternoon practice of *passeggiata*, a lovely way of families strolling about.

The youngsters were lively, noisy, showing off, speeding along on Lambrettas, the boys shouting endearments and the young girls showing off their legs and long hair worn loose, in plaits or ponytails, looking absolutely stunning. But then so did Pia in her stylish Ellesse leggings and top, complimented by a designer cap. She sighed with pleasure and thought how easy, relaxed, and enjoyable life in Italy seemed to be.

As the shadows grew longer, Pia took another look at the wonderful Cathedral Metropolitan di San Pietro, admiring the detail of the building; inside, the choir was practicing, filling the square with a series of lovely melodies.

The young woman then strolled into a delicatessen, where she purchased a large basket full of delicacies she planned to give to the monks of the monastery. Her cousin Maya had kindly arranged for her to stay for three nights to enjoy luxurious accommodation, outstanding food and service, excellent sports facilities, opportunities for horse riding, and the wonderful surrounding countryside.

Chapter 20

Exposures: Switzerland and Italy

Anton Gruber was worried; the nice Miss Marinello just did not seem the same these days, not nearly as friendly and never chatty like she used to be. In fact, when the deputy concierge tried to engage her with some friendly tale, she glared at him wordlessly and swept into the lift to her apartment.

Miss von Gunten, Miss Marinello's cousin and housekeeper during her frequent absence, suddenly appeared; she glared at Anton, gave him some instructions, and then disappeared out of the portal. Strangely enough, it reminded him of the similar way her normally chatty cousin had behaved earlier.

Adding to that, he found some mysterious objects and parcels in the young lady's storage area; it puzzled Anton and made him feel he was missing something really important. He decided to investigate after Miss Marinello left for the airport. Once Miss von Gunten finished her duties and left the building, he went to the garage.

Anton looked around the garage and found Maya von Gunten's car, which she had left for routine maintenance. When he opened the driver's door, a strange chemical smell hit his senses, not at all like the delightful fragrance of Miss Marinello's car.

"Ok, Miss Hoity Toity, what's your game?" Anton asked as he explored the various compartments, which contained simple girly bits and bobs. Then he said, "Now, Miss von Gunten, what have we got here? Parking receipts, but in between, a receipt from Huniger Iron Mongers? Can't see what she bought, it's all in code, but over eight hundred franks?"

Anton decided to take another look at Miss Marinello's personal storage area in the attic, for which he had a key. So did Miss von Gunten, of course, and Anton had found evidence of her hidden secret containers in the past. "Ok, Concierge, let's have a closer look. So where is VG's special rollaway and her secret box? Here, underneath those blankets, there's a torn-up piece of paper; it seems to be part of some military communication. Bingo, Anton, full marks, and I will now add two documents to my sturdy box, which includes several other objects."

Meanwhile, Colonel Burki's investigators, Sergeant Rita and Corporal Bruno, led by Professor Tobias Berger, were on the trail of the traitor who had alerted Milton Adams and thwarted the special forces raid. Their inquiries also focused on whoever was the lethal, sharp-shooting individual with a deadly crossbow.

Their inquiries started at the military base, where they reviewed the profiles of all military personnel at the compound, including those working part-time. This thorough investigation became the cornerstone of their dossier, including six individuals who warranted further scrutiny.

After a full day of investigating, Bruno and Rita went to the Roxy nightclub, which was in full swing with several hundred youngsters, businessmen and -women, soldiers, and academics, enjoying a lively night out. The two young officers loved to dance. This evening's mission was specifically targeted to identify possible sources of information about recent events. Bruno and Rita were in comfortable casual attire but also suitable to rumble in case of the occasional fracas that sometime occurred. The two of them were very close friends and loved to dance, and Bruno's hand occasionally slipped underneath Rita's blouse, making her giggle.

As they enjoyed the moment, they quietly moved closer to a group of raucous youngsters who were discussing what happened in the mountains and speculated about the identity of the crossbow assassin.

"I saw someone running from the military base with a backpack round about the time when all this happened," said a young boy.

Another chipped in, "And I know one of the assistants who comes from somewhere near Zurich."

The Molehill

More information emerged as an argument developed within the group.

One of the youngsters said, "I hate that arrogant cow; she does not give her name but her boyfriend is a farmer outside a place called Baden."

Bruno led his partner away from the loud youngsters and said, "Rita, I am sure you are working all this out in your lovely, cheeky creative way. Let's go somewhere far more relaxed and mull it over, whilst we enjoy one of our special evenings. Your place or mine?"

The following morning, Professor Berger complimented the two young officers, who glanced affectionately at each other, on their detailed report about the Roxy discoveries.

"Now looking through your records, I have come across the specialist female assistant who seems to be employed on specific operations. Furthermore, she seems to have a connection with a certain Bernhard Luthi, who is a communications expert at the military base.

"So now, Rita and Bruno, we are off to see Mr Ueli Amberg near Fislisbach, not far from the old town of Baden, because he has a link to Maya von Gunten, one of your possible suspects."

The farm in the middle of the countryside was neat and tidy, and the young farmer was visibly proud of his business and took great care to show the three representatives of the government around.

After a while, the professor delicately mentioned Amberg's girlfriend, Maya von Gunten; Ueli's look of distress showed how worried he was.

He said, "Maya disappeared quite some time ago and has not answered my messages. Then I contacted the posh fashion store in Baden where she worked, but they said she has not been in touch for over a week."

The professor thanked Ueli and promised to keep him updated when there were any positive developments.

The next stop of the inquiry led the team to Maya von Gunten's cousin, Pia Marinello, at the luxurious business and apartment complex in the old town of Baden. Anton Gruber, the lively porter and deputy concierge, confirmed that neither Miss van Gunten nor her cousin, Miss Marinello, had been seen for several days. The formidable Anton proved to be a fount of information with a torrent of gossip, a sturdy box full of evidence, and perfect leads to find the hardware store where the crossbow

Kurt Hafner

bolts had been purchased. He also provided a further link to the military base.

Around 240 miles south of Baden, Pia Marinello enjoyed a leisurely morning, window shopping, buying some treats and a new hat, and sampling different food and beverages in the ancient town of Bologna. She chose one of the best restaurants and ordered a refreshing lunch of Vitello Tonnato, the traditional combination of thinly sliced veal in a creamy tuna fish sauce, followed by fresh figs, a variety of local cheeses, delicious wine, an espresso, and a plate of Amaretti biscuits.

Then a little later, she walked back to the hotel, finished packing, and got dressed for her visit to the monastery, which her cousin Maya had so kindly organized.

As she waited in the lobby, sipping sparkling mineral water, the concierge approached and said, "Your wonderful transport has arrived, *Signorina* Marinello; may I help you with your luggage?"

"Yes, Alfredo, and thank you for a splendid three days at your lovely hotel."

What Pia had not expected was to see a pony and trap waiting for her outside the hotel. A tall, flamboyant monk approached her and introduced himself as her host, Brother Anselmo, who gallantly helped her to the comfortable seat at the back of the buggy.

After a charming ride through the countryside, past vineyards, grazing sheep, woodland, and olive plantations, they arrived at the monastery, where Pia was greeted by a small man dressed in morning suit, who bowed and courteously said, "Welcome, Miss Marinello, my name is Musgrove, and I shall be at your service during your stay. It is our enormous pleasure to welcome you to our modest home. I invite you to follow me to your suite."

Pia was surprised by the very dark long corridors and the chanting monks; she saw several of them scurrying around, in and out of the many doors along this long walkway. Musgrove gave a running commentary about the building and the various locations. As they reached the end of the corridor, Musgrove demonstrably knocked on a giant wooden double door, which opened by an electronic device.

Inside, the scenario completely changed, as they stepped into a lavish

The Molehill

glass-enclosed reception area and through another electronic door onto a wide, carpeted staircase. Pia counted two flights of twelve steps each and concluded they were underground.

"This way, Miss," Musgrove said, as he pointed to another corridor, this one light and luxurious. "And here we are, your suite is number 7, right here."

The strange man opened the door.

Pia was astounded by the magnificent layout of her accommodation, including spacious and comfortable living areas, double bedroom, separate dressing room, a mini kitchen, a fully stocked bar with a vast range of beverages and wine, a lavish bathroom, and a miniature swimming pool. Although there were no actual windows, the design included artificial views of countryside, the sea, wildlife, and mountains, giving the impression of open spaces. The air-conditioning was quite superb, with a light fragrance of autumnal flowers.

As Pia quietly explored her luxurious environment, there was a knock on the door; a monk and a waitress rolled in a table laden with delicacies, a bottle of champagne, and a pot of steaming coffee. There was an ornate gold rimmed card saying "Enjoy your stay, Miss Marinello; take time to relax. Dinner will be served at eight o'clock."

Pia had a snack and a glass of champagne, then decided that a siesta was in order, as there was plenty of time for a comfortable forty winks. Later, she took a bath before getting dressed, and after, she tried the door leading into the corridor, but she could not open it.

"Good evening, Miss Marinello," boomed a voice from the giant television screen, which had magically sprung into life, showing beautiful landscapes, wildlife, and flowers. "We hope you are enjoying our facilities; please don't be alarmed by the closed door. Our superb security arrangements simply ensure that you are safe and comfortable; we look forward to escorting you to dinner."

Milton Adams had watched every movement and plenty of closeups of the new arrival and said appreciatively, "Yes, Musgrove, she'll do fine; quite pretty, and a decent figure. Let's fit her in after the local girl, Melissa."

Chapter 21

Into the Wilderness: Colorado

The lecture hall at the University of Colorado was packed and completely full of students, faculty, civic leaders, and eminent guests. The audience of more than three hundred were enthralled by the dynamic presentation about the thrill, excitement, and danger of fighting crime and subversive threats, wherever they may occur.

"And so my friends," Commander Belinda Carrington concluded, "what an enormous pleasure this morning and such a privilege for me to address exceptionally gifted students, brilliant faculty, superb leadership, and your eminent guests. My compliments on your perceptive interactions, and thank you for the stimulus of your lively, creative contributions today. My very best wishes to all of you."

The audience rose in a standing ovation for Belinda, who looked stunning in her sportive House of Bruar country attire. The master of ceremony raised his hand for silence, and the dean formally thanked Belinda for her enthralling contribution by enriching the background and knowledge of the university. He also announced that Commander Harrington would be awarded an honorary doctorate by the university.

"Congratulations, Belinda," Professor Campbell said. "And guess who is here and wants to compliment you on your fantastic presentation? None other than your friend, Fenella Hardwick, Rolf Brenner Inc's celebrated lawyer."

Fenella looked glamorous wearing an ornate Indian dress and headband; she beamed, hugged Belinda, and said, "Congratulations,

The Molehill

Lindy, so loved your fantastic presentation, and my compliments on your selection as one of the top crimefighters in the world."

Finally, to conclude the proceedings, the two senior students and Fenella handed Belinda a miniature statue of Ralphie, the university's buffalo mascot, which she had earlier seen running about in his compound.

After a delicious lunch, it was time for Belinda to depart into the wilderness, starting with a mountain bike ride to the top of Lookout Mountain. Her luggage, saddle, climbing gear, and a tent were in the helicopter, ready for her camp at a secret place in the mountains, where her two helpers would establish her base camp.

Later, Fenella Hardwick left for Denver Airport, and as she recalled his welcome on her arrival from La Guardia, she enjoyed the familiar feeling of warmth and excitement that always engulfed her in anticipation of seeing Lord Britton. Not just seeing him, but this time spending five days together in the exclusive mountain lodge.

There were plenty of admiring glances at the lovely young woman in traditional glamorous Indian dress and headband. She went into the United Airlines VIP lounge and enjoyed some refreshments while she studied her dossier about the latest incidents that had affected Rolf Brenner.

The murder of her client's wealthy investors and sponsors in Manhattan had been cleared up by Lieutenant Leroy Simmons and his team, and they also solved the attack on Lord Britton after his arrival from London. However, there was insufficient progress about the devastating timebomb at a popular restaurant in Queens. Although some arrests had been made, the remainder of the gang presented a major challenge for Lieutenant Simmons and Sergeant Raymond Kenny, who was leading the team to round up the culprits.

Further south, around Florida's barrier islands, some rather amateurish attempts to unnerve Rolf, Sabine, their children, and Samantha had been dealt with by the local police force and Coast Guard. Sam had shown commendable initiative by enlisting the help of two friends, a Princeton graduate and an Australian resident, to find the miscreants. The resourceful trio were remarkably successful and able to produce a detailed dossier of information for the local chief of police, Joyce Allan, who used their invaluable guide in rounding up and convicting the group of hoodlums and miscreants.

In Switzerland, Fenella's friend, Colonel Peter Burki, head of the Swiss Secret Service. was on the trail of a traitor working for the unknown assailant, who wanted to weaken her client's business and then to acquire its valuable microelectronics, intellect, and factories. On a more sinister note, the Swiss were also on the trail of an assassin whose weapon of choice was a deadly accurate crossbow. And finally, an investigation had been started between the Swiss and the Italian special forces about some mysterious activities in connection with an ancient monastery near Bologna.

Suddenly, Fenella detected a presence, a change in her surroundings, and then felt a calming hand on her shoulder. This was all she wanted, as Nigel Britton hugged her, looked into her eyes, and said, "Hello, gorgeous. Fenella darling, you simply look stunning and ready to sort out whatever you have been plotting."

The glamorous young lawyer greeted him with a mischievous smile and said, "Well, my Lord, I thought I had better be ready for you with my update about the colonies and our clients."

Nigel chuckled, took her in his arms, and whispered, "As long, my darling, as you are ready for me and never mind your brilliant dossier, which can wait for much later."

In the meantime, Belinda was well on the way towards the top of Lookout Mountain, pedalling energetically around all the many bends and an ever increasing and challenging incline. She made one stop to rehydrate with the refreshing local mineral water and then continued to power up towards the top of the mountain, where she secured her bike near the café and souvenir shop.

After a brief climb to the top, she paused at Buffalo Bill's lovely grave; it was the ideal place to reflect on the beauty around her. She quietly sat on a bench with her own very personal thoughts and some wonderful memories of the many magical moments she had enjoyed with the love of her life, Major Duncan Stewart of the Scots Guards, who was tragically killed by a sniper in Kosovar.

After a while, she felt at ease, refreshed, and ready to explore the beautiful surroundings, with wonderful views of the scenery and the mighty mountains beyond. As she did so, she noticed a bald eagle, which circled way above against a flawless, dark blue sky. So perfect for her to reflect and nurture the fond memory of her late fiancé.

Come on, Duncan, she thought, *simply soar in the sky, just like this majestic eagle and I will always cheer you on.* At that moment, a thoughtful smile lightened up her face, as she wiped a few tears from her eyes.

Soon after, her helicopter appeared; it circled the area, signalled her, and then landed a short distance away. Brad Coulter, one of her organization's senior members responsible for the USA, had arranged for one of his agents to be her guard, minder, and pilot, and Belinda was soon on the way to her secret camp in the mountains, with the view of the spectacular wilderness from the copilot's seat.

They flew precariously, zigzagging in between gigantic rock formations for a while, then over a small mountain lake and eventually a green valley, with Belinda's Cherokee assistants waving them to a perfect place to land. The young woman, Chenoa, meaning Dove, and her companion, a boy called Waya, meaning Wolf, welcomed their mistress and her guard to her remarkable camp; they had constructed it from natural materials, which made it almost invisible to the untrained eye.

The neighing of some horses and the welcoming bark of two dogs (called Yona, meaning Bear, and Onacona, meaning white owl, in addition to a goshawk called Wohaly, meaning Eagle) completed the domestic population to guard Belinda. The enticing aroma of roast mountain hare and snow partridge was just a prelude to a delicious dinner the young Indians had prepared, and after a refreshing swim in the lake, Belinda went into her private part of the camp to sleep.

Early the next morning, Belinda completed her regular exercises; she ran five miles, reconnoitred the environment, said hello to a mighty moose, enjoyed a swim in the lake, and then with a ravenous appetite ate a hearty breakfast. Soon she waved good bye to Brad's agent, as the helicopter flew past before leaving for Boulder. Her horse was saddled and ready for the next stage of her adventure: a long trek through the mountains towards the plains and the forests of Colorado. Later on, as she rested, leaning against an ancient pine near a brook for her horse to drink, she enjoyed the delicious food her assistants had packed, including smoked fish and some of the previous evening's roast poultry.

She drifted into a wonderfully relaxed state of mind, reminiscing, reflecting, and enjoying the soothing sounds of insects, birds, the bubbling of the brook nearby, and the gentle breeze in the trees. When she woke up from her refreshing slumber, she looked forward to returning back to her mountain camp, as her horse trotted through the shrubbery.

Riding through the forest was also a perfect time to reflect on the recent subversive criminal activities and to analyse the success which had already been achieved in Manhattan by Lieutenant Simmons's team, led by Sergeants Ray Kenny and Lara Pregowski.

This now left the challenges of the bomb attack in Queens to be resolved by Lieutenant Simmons, his two sergeants, and their team. Further afield in Switzerland, Colonel Peter Burki and his brigade were pursuing a crossbow assassin and a traitor who had infiltrated their organization.

Finally, not too far away from Switzerland in northern Italy, there were indications of a serious conspiracy and an underground head office of the personification of evil, Milton Adams, which urgently required investigation.

As Belinda gradually increased her tempo and galloped back to camp, she felt so privileged to have a few days' rest, but she also felt excited at perhaps resolving these fascinating challenges.

Just then, she heard someone talking, which immediately put her on high alert.

"These stupid American horses are useless and don't understand what I tell them to do, not like our white Camarque horses."

A typical argument soon developed between the three French individuals Belinda had overheard at Heathrow and then on her flight to Denver. She quietly withdrew, contacted her guard with the co-ordinate of the trio's location, and trotted away towards the camp.

However, as she came across a ridge, she surveyed the terrain and spotted a disturbance in the forest on the opposite side of the valley. She noticed a slim individual clad in black with a hood who ran up the slope

The Molehill

and disappeared into the dense undergrowth of the forest. She decided to investigate and signalled her guard.

Once the pilot landed, the two of them plus the young Cherokee, who was an expert tracker, set off across the valley, where they reached a footpath with evidence of two mountain bike tracks, which they followed.

"Looks like a couple taking a rest near the brook down below," Belinda said.

But instead of happy sounds and laughter, which they expected, they found the two bikes in the brook below and, far worse, their two occupants sprawled some distance apart from each other at the bottom of the hill.

"Shhh, quiet; you look for the assassin Waya," Belinda said as she drew her handgun and hunting knife. "Aw, poor youngsters, a boy and a girl."

Each had been killed by a crossbow bolt.

"Red alert," Belinda messaged. "UK HQ, Brad Coulter, Nigel Britton, Fenella Hardwick, Colonel Burki, mobilizing the cavalry, and woe betide the black-clad assassin."

A wonderful leisurely day had therefore developed into the prelude of a situation which would tax Belinda's ultimate resourcefulness, stamina, resilience, and her razor-sharp mind.

Chapter 22

The Swiss Connection: Switzerland

The meeting in Colonel Peter Burki's office started at 08.30; the magnificent parliament building had wonderful views of the old town of Bern, the River Aare that wound itself around the capital of Switzerland, and the snow-covered mountains beyond.

The team had enjoyed an early breakfast of freshly baked ham croissants, Gruyere cheese tartlets, the famous local butter pretzels, fresh grape juice, aromatic brewed coffee, and plenty of sparkling mineral water.

Peter stood up and declared, his voice booming in his typical Bern-bear accent, "Well, ladies and gentlemen, I hope we all enjoyed a sumptuous breakfast because, believe me, today we will need all our energy, creativity, and intuition. This is it, and with all the information now available, we must develop a detailed plan to close down this evil organisation, once and for all.

"My compliments to Professor Tobias Berger, and to you, my two agents, Sergeant Rita and Corporal Bruno, for your discoveries of some fascinating links in Switzerland and reaching all the way to Italy, which may well be the key to unlocking this mystery. So Toby, please provide us with the details the three of you discovered."

The professor stood up; he looked impressive with his snow-white hair, and he had replaced his traditional farmer's outfit and jaunty hat with a formal suit and tie. He began, "Our investigation started at the military base in Thun, after the regrettable incident of the crossbow assassin, who tragically killed Sergeant Armin, one of the colonel's best officers, and severely wounded Corporal Sarah Manser, who thankfully is well on the way to recovery and may soon rejoin the team in the hunt of the perpetrator.

"Our condolences go out to Sergeant Armin's family," Toby said. "They are receiving support and counselling, and our very best wishes for Sarah's recovery. Now the initial investigation was conducted by Rita and Bruno, whom I did not have to persuade to enter the wilderness of the Roxy Club, where they are well known." The professor smiled. "Whilst dancing the night away, they found some information which on the following day led us to the village of Fislisbach near Baden, where a local farmer was desperately worried about his girlfriend, Maya von Gunten, who appeared to have disappeared from the face of the earth. Now I would like Rita, who was the chief investigator, to tell us about her fascinating discoveries."

Rita looked fetching, wearing a tight Ellesse blouse (Bruno's favourite), a smart navy pleated skirt, and knee-length boots. She smiled and began, "The farmer, Ueli, gave us a number of clues which led us to question the supercilious manageress of the exclusive store, where his girlfriend worked part time. The lady simply confirmed this employee had disappeared after buying some top-class military clothes and mountaineering gear. Ueli, who joined us at that stage, then led us to a business and apartment complex, where the elusive Maya apparently was the part-time housekeeper for her cousin, Pia Marinello, a senior flight attendant of the national airline.

"Now this was when the investigation got really interesting because Anton Gruber, the porter of the building, proved to be a fountain of information. He observed Pia and Maya, analysed their behaviour, and discovered a number of similarities within their ways and characters. He also discovered Maya's secrets, especially, receipts from a local hardware outlet, part of a military communication, and most importantly a hidden store, where she had placed incriminating materials for safe keeping. Anton indicated either of them might be the housekeeper or the flight attendant because of their physical similarity, so may I please invite Bruno to explain our dramatic conclusions."

Bruno, looking smart in light slacks and a navy blazer, pointed to the screen, which showed a map that highlighted Switzerland, Italy, and the United States. He explained, "Let us remain in Switzerland at this stage, where we have identified the crossbow assassin as Maya von Gunten. Not only is she the killer but also the impersonator of Pia as a senior flight attendant. Both women are of an identical size and similar facial features. While von Gunten was housekeeper during Marinello's frequent and long absences abroad, she had all the opportunity to study the airline's instructions and guidelines, and of course to acquire her initial uniform.

"Now this is where the situation becomes both complex and dangerous because Maya, now operating as Pia, a senior cabin attendant, set up an elaborate plan to eliminate her cousin by treating her to three days at an ancient Italian monastery on the hills above Bologna. In doing so, Pia will be delivered into the perverted claws of Milton Brown. Now may I please introduce my own cousin, Enrico, of the elite Swiss grenadiers based at Losone, in the Swiss Italian county of Ticino. Enrico, *prego*."

"Thank you, Colonel, for your invitation, and yes, your Pia Marinello is in mortal danger because her cousin has paved the way for her demise. Maya is an operative of Milton Adams, who is determined to take over Rolf and Sabine Brenner's prosperous factories. On his behalf, she operates as an assassin and impersonates a senior flight attendant.

"Now, I am glad to introduce one of my best friends, Capitano Bianca Tomassini, who is a member of the famous mountain corps of the Italian army, the Carabinieri; thank you, Colonel, for inviting her to join us with the most fascinating details and a creative proposal as to how the enemy base in Italy could be destroyed."

"*Prego*, Bianca." An impressive young woman in military uniform came onto the stage, saluted, and then said in perfect English, "Colonel Burki, ladies and gentlemen, you may think, how lovely, quaint, and endearing this old monastery is, with melodic bells, the monks' religious activities, the choir, and humble staff going about their business.

"But let us not be deceived, because alerted by Enrico, I managed to identify a major threat and a most sinister development at this seemingly innocent monastery. Unbeknown to anyone, there is below the ancient building a labyrinth of caves and caverns, an underground lake, and at the outflow a massive waterfall.

"But far more sinister, the monastery is managed by Brother Anselmo, a cunning and powerful monk who has eliminated the influence of the old ailing abbot, who is contented to remain in his cell for most of the time. The Crow, as he is known, rules the monks with an iron fist and made them completely subservient to him by eliminating any of those who were not compliant to his commands. He then became a member of Milton Adams's organisation, converted the caves into the most lavish and luxurious premises in secrecy, totally hidden away and completely soundproofed, so no one can hear what evil deeds are taking place underground.

"My secret informant, Brother Ricardo, a young monk I knew at school, is obviously operating in a highly dangerous situation. He has confirmed that Pia Marinello is currently a resident in a most luxurious suite but unable to leave her assigned quarters; she is virtually a prisoner. Milton Adams's new base and his evil organisation are functioning in so many different ways. Thank you for providing me with this opportunity of adding to the background of what will be a fascinating campaign."

At this point, Colonel Burki rose and announced, "Thank you very much, Capitano, for your superb contribution, and Professor, for your lively descriptions. Everyone, congratulations on your splendid discoveries. This is a perfect time for us to take a break before enjoying lunch at the Bellevue Palace, where the maître d' and executive chef have prepared a delicious meal for us.

"This afternoon, we will resume our preparations and get to work on our objective of eliminating Adams and his mob. Formulating this plan is a matter of priority. I salute all of you and look forward to this crucial session this afternoon."

The participants gave him a warm round of applause in prelude to the excitement of creating solutions to the threats and dangers ahead.

The buffet was delicious, with a perfect selection of Swiss specialities and local wines, completed by a selection of cheese and a superb chestnut meringue gateau. The view over the old town, the river, and the Alps was magnificent, and the discussions around the table focused on the task ahead. Soon the animated group returned to the parliament building, ready for action.

Peter Burki resumed the meeting by announcing that Maya von Gunten had flown to Miami, impersonating Pia Marinello. After checking in at the superb Miami beach hotel, she had suddenly vanished, including all her luggage and belongings, leaving her colleagues high and dry.

The colonel, pointing to the change of images on the screen, said, "The traitor then appeared on the high plain of Colorado, where I just received a report about two crossbow fatalities. This matter is now being handled by Commander Carrington, whose outbound holiday was disrupted, supported by Lord Britton and Fenella Hardwick, who also were on a break in Boulder. Our local agent Brad Coulter and his team are mobilizing the necessary resources to support a major operation.

"So, team, we all are now well nourished and refreshed after a most delicious lunch. The USA incident is being expertly handled; I don't want us to be distracted from our major task, which is to snuff out the threat in Bologna, eliminate this evil organisation, and rescue Pia Marinello. We must use all our expertise and creativity to prepare a perfect plan, which must be completed by eight o'clock tonight. Good luck, boys and girls. We will declare a red alert and move on to battle stations tomorrow."

The senior members took the lead and focussed on the different key elements of the major operation. As the afternoon shadows grew longer, the specialists coordinated their recommendations and informed Colonel Burki they were ready to present him with a master plan to destroy Milton Adams's organisation.

Professor Berger came onto the stage and pointed to the illuminated screen, which displayed a map of Switzerland, Italy, and North America.

"Let me give you a brief summary of the changes which affect our target. It appears there has been an exodus from the secret and sinister organisation below the Santa Lucia Monastery above Bologna. First of all, Colonel Tarrant recently left Bologna and flew to Denver with a German miscreant, Gerhard Berger. He was soon followed by the formidable Hannah Gerber, who has also remained on our radar.

"To summarise, this now leaves the residents below the monastery as Milton Adams, Musgrove, Brother Anselmo, a young female Italian prisoner, and Pia Marinello, who seems to be well treated by her hosts but unable to leave her expansive and luxurious suite. She is in severe danger from the sinister attentions of Adams. I will now invite Captain Tomassini to present her creative proposal; the total situation in Italy can be resolved in three stages. Please, Bianca."

The young Italian officer adjusted the live presentation on the screen, which now showed a sequence of three operations: "Priority number one must be to free Pia from her virtual prison, and to this end, my informant, Brother Ricardo, has found a secret passageway, through which he plans to lead Pia to safety; she will be handed over to members of Colonel Burki's team, supported by an elite squad of Carabinieris.

"The second phase of the operation will be the destruction of the lavish underground locations; we can do so with the help of Mother Nature. There is a small gate at the outlet from the overflowing mountain lake. This gate is part of a system to direct a strong vortex of water into a narrow channel, where it is directed to flow alongside and then merge with the waterfall. Our calculations show the enormous power of this water can destroy whatever is in the way, starting with all the constructions on the three levels of the evil organisation's locations."

"Thank you, Capitano" said the professor, "and now the third and final phase will be to track Maya von Gunten, who apparently has left Colorado and is on the way to Bologna. We must identify her whereabouts, flush her out, and terminate her operations.

"Finally, please allow me to conclude a successful day and what I recommend as a perfect master plan," said the professor, "which I recommend for adoption and to be launched as a matter of priority.

The colonel smiled and announced, "My sincere compliments Toby, Captain Tomassini, Sergeant Liechti, Corporal Hintermann, and all your colleagues. We start at 2 a.m. tomorrow. Good luck, and good hunting."

Chapter 23

Red Alert: Colorado and New York

Belinda's red alert triggered a series of nonstop activities; her guard immediately started the helicopter and was joined by a squad of agents; they rose from their base in the valley and flew to the top of the incline to the high plains. In continuous contact with Belinda, the pilot glided along the edge of the forest and finally rose sharply, turned left, swooped down, and landed in a clearing at the base of the hill, where the victims of the crossbow assassin had been found. This exclusive area was now guarded by Brad Coulter and three of his agents, fully armed, ready for their mission of hunting down the assassin who had killed the two young cyclists.

The squad, guided by the expert Cherokee tracker Waya, then followed the trail of the three individuals on horseback, who had behaved in a most obnoxious way in the café and giftshop at the top of Lookout Mountain. They were obviously French and according to their Provençale accents, spoke very broken English. They arrogantly maintained everything in France was so much superior to anything they experienced abroad. The three riders charged across their path, whooping and yelling aggressively. Two bursts of gunfire from Brad's agents chased them into the wilderness and up a steep incline, and then they disappeared.

In the meantime, Lord Britton responded to the red alert by enlisting the help of Professor Campbell and his team to join him and Fenella

The Molehill

Hardwick for a war council. He also contacted his influential colleagues on Wall Street, who alerted their international security experts by video link.

Finally, the fourth response to the red alert reached the consolidated summer camp of the Colorado-based Cherokee tribes, where the drums resounded from the rocky faces surrounding the plain and forests, signalling a war council was due to start.

Unbeknown to any of these groups, two senior members of Milton Adams's organisation and a new German recruit secretly arrived in New York and booked three suites at the Four Seasons Hotel. The mystery team consisted of Colonel Tarrant, his sinister personal assistant, Hannah Gerber, and one of her recruits, Johann Albrecht. Soon after their arrival, they met in a private room as Tarrant took the chair with the following statement:

"Right, our mission is to destroy as many elements of Rolf Brenner's organisation, starting with his trusted team, who all seem to be on a break in Colorado. Before doing so, we will deal with Elna Petroni, who used to work with Christopher Huntingdon in Queens. As you know, he was already eliminated for his team's incompetence, and the same fate now awaits Petroni, which Albrecht will arrange.

"Now for our plan to eliminate the Colorado-based Rolf Brenner supporters, we have plenty of resources at our disposal, including those members of the Cockney Demons who are not in jail and our three French hitmen. Your secret mole and sharp shooting spy, Gerber, unfortunately disappeared and appears to be on the way to Bologna. Now let's go and hit the Brenners. So here's the plan: …"

In the meantime, across the Brooklyn Bridge, Valentino Cuccione was puzzled, He was earning loads of money, of course, but what worried him was that no one had made arrangements to collect the painting and three drawings, which he disliked intensely but had dutifully completed as instructed. So where was that mysterious lady with her terse telephone instructions to let him know where he should hand over his four pictures?

The lady in question was also on a mission and had a sinister plan of her own: to kill Valentino and his girlfriend Orsina, because the Italian painter had destroyed her ingeniously brilliant plan. Her instructions by the master were to blow up at least a dozen high-ranking officials, police officers, and wealthy business owners, some of whom were closely linked to Rolf Brenner's organisation. Instead, Valentino Cuccione's favourite waitress and the headwaiter had been blown into smithereens and others injured. Elna Petroni and her boyfriend, Richard Huntingdon, got the blame. To top it all, Richard had been killed on a waterfall in northern Italy. Yes, she would wreak revenge on those who had destroyed her credibility and were somehow responsible for the death of her Christopher.

Elna marched along the main road, carrying Christopher's umbrella, which hid a bayonet with an expertly poisoned tip; in her bag was some rope and a special explosive device. She planned to start her revenge by first of all killing Orsina Capellini, Valentino's girlfriend. Thereafter, she would despatch Valentino Cuccione and finally blow up Orsina's parents' delicatessen. Yes, revenge was sweet, and soon she reached the underground car park, ready to drive to her first destination.

In order to achieve two flawless murders and take revenge in the most dramatic style, Elna had recruited the three remaining Cockney Demons, who seemed lost without their leader, who had been arrested with several colleagues and charged with murder. Her new recruits prepared a Fiat transit van and were waiting for her in the underground car park below a business and apartment complex.

The NYPD had kept Elna and her team under close observation for several days and were at this time not far away with a small group of specialists.

Sergeant Lara Pregowski adjusted the focus of her binoculars and electronic hearing device. "She's on a mission, Ray," Lara said to Sergeant Kenny, who studied the relevant image on his iPad. "Let's wait till she drives off and have her followed by our two specialists who are lying in wait."

Elna stepped out of the elevator at the ground level, where her car was parked. She noticed a shadow disappearing up the stairs; she frowned but thought it was most likely a driver who had parked a car and hurried into the building above. She carefully packed her special goods in their designated place in the car and reviewed her plan of action with the three thugs, who were seated in the rear of the van.

The Molehill

She waited for a while, smoking a cigarette, and once her mind was crystal clear, she shouted, "Action stations," started the engine, drove up the ramp, and stopped at the main road.

Johann Albrecht, who had watched the car park below the office and apartment building from his vantage point in the park opposite, pushed the plunger. The red car exploded with a thunderous noise, bursting into flames; it was rocked and totally destroyed by a secondary explosion caused by Elna's lethal bomb, which was destined for Orsina's parents' deli.

Not far away, Valentino Cuccione heard the enormous explosions; he immediately grabbed his camera, ran round the corner, and started to photograph the carnage and debris. Then the two police motorbikes, several squad cars, ambulances, the fire brigade, and senior police officers took charge of the situation.

Albrecht cheered and bellowed out a German marching song as he charged across the top of the ridge, overlooking the disaster area below, and congratulating himself on eliminating Elna Petroni in such a brilliant way. He could hardly wait for Colonel Tarrant and Hannah Gerber's compliments and rewards.

Albrecht skipped up the stairs to the first-floor mezzanine of the Four Seasons and went into the conference room, where he had been instructed to report. What he had not expected and what shocked him was the stony silence and the aggressive facial expressions, as Hannah shouted, "Another major cock-up, Albrecht, you absolutely useless idiot."

Tarrant stood in front of him and said, "So you eliminated Petroni, but in your stupidity, you also killed the three remaining Cockney Demons, who were in the back of the van; they were our eyes and ears."

Hannah Gerber hissed, "Transfer to Colorado for you, boy, and hope you get an Indian arrow bang where it terminates you."

Chapter 24

The Cherokee Solution: Colorado

"This is our most crucial period, Sabine," Rolf told his wife. "It's a special moment we planned to result in a triumphant move forward, and yet, my darling, I sense great danger ahead."

Sabine caressed his face with her hand.

"Come on, Rolfi, so unlike you, but remember, Nigel and Fenella are waiting for us, and Belinda is securing our event on the high plains, although she should really be on holiday."

In the meantime, Rolf's private jet was on the final approach to a small airport just outside Boulder. The cabin attendants collected the champagne glasses and the ornate plates on which exquisite canapes had been served to the company's senior managers and forty of their most important customers and suppliers.

As the aircraft slowly taxied to the terminal, Sabine Brenner welcomed the group to the company's annual business conference on the high plains of Colorado, saying, "A fleet of limousines will transport you to the St Julien Hotel and Spa. Then after we have settled into our suites, you will find a comprehensive programme for our three-day event, and then we will be driven to a lodge in the forest behind the university for an informal dinner."

As the evening dawned, a fleet of horse-drawn carriages arrived at the front of the hotel, ready to carry the guests through the forest. Soon the enticing aroma of grilled beef gave the delegates an indication of the delicious food that would be served. A country and western band was also in action to welcome them and set the scene for the evening.

This gathering underneath a starlit sky was certainly a wonderful event, starting with cocktails, followed by a selection of prime beef, grilled mountain trout, and rustic local specialities. There was plenty of Californian champagne, fine wine, desserts, and local cheeses. Then there were a few local announcements and finally a rousing speech by Lord Britton.

As some of the couples danced the evening away, others gathered in informal groups, enjoying the sound of the band or taking the opportunity for a leisurely stroll through the woods. This was until one of the local police officers, who had been on security duty, discreetly handed a note to Logan Thompson, the chief of police, who was a guest at the party.

Logan alerted Rolf, Sabine, Nigel, and Fenella Hardwick, and they reviewed the information which indicated a crossbow assassin was on the loose and might strike anywhere without notice. They decided that although they were well protected by the local police, they should drastically increase security. In the meantime, however, they were happy to let the party take its course; after it concluded, the guests returned to their luxurious hotel.

When they got back, some of the guests remained in the lounge or at the bar for a while, but they soon drifted off to their suites for a peaceful and restful good night. All the suites became silent, the lights were progressively extinguished, and the only audible sounds were the calls of some owls, the occasional howl of a distant coyote, and the chirping of crickets.

Things were quiet until half past three, when a thunderous roar from the hillside awakened everyone in the hotel. Brad Coulter, Belinda Carrington's senior USA agent, shot out of bed and contacted the local police. Their network soon established there had been an attack on a fire station on the road to Lookout Mountain; access to the summit was temporarily blocked.

Most of the guests were unaware of the drama, but the general manager of the hotel sent cards under everyone's door with a brief explanation of the disturbance. He also announced a midnight feast was available for anyone feeling peckish.

The second alert was received at seven the following morning, with the most dreadful news of an attack on several tourists and their Cherokee guides, who were killed on the way to the high plains. There were fourteen casualties or severely wounded; the assailants were three white males on horseback, a tall military man and his assistant, who spoke with a German accent, and a striking, assertive female.

When the news broke, the hunt for the perpetrators was already well on the way, led by Belinda Carrington, Brad Coulter, and several agents who had been summoned following the attack on the fire station.

At the same time, a powerful squad of Cherokee warriors had been assigned by their senior council to assist Belinda and help to bring the killers to justice, supported by the four best trackers of their tribe, whose skills and expertise were supported by their specially trained coyote-style dogs. They were known as the best scouts in the world.

Rolf and Sabine Brenner were in session with Lord Brittan and Fenella Hardwick, discussing the risks of their original plan of flying the delegates with their fleet of helicopters to the picturesque clearing amongst the forests and rocks of the high plains and a luxurious marquee, styled like a village of tepees. It had been set up with local food and beverages, and hosted by a stylish group of Cherokee university graduates. However, the team unanimously decided to relocate the conference to the safety of the hotel.

The delegates were treated to a lavish breakfast and then invited into the luxurious room where round tables and light refreshments were ready for the opening session of the conference. Rolf Brenner was in great form and delivered a stirring speech, which he started with a precise summary of the two security incidents; he reassured the delegates and continued, "I am pleased to confirm that our investigations are supported by some formidable experts and international crimefighters. We are therefore well protected, and we may therefore be confident of a glittering future for our business and yours."

The delegates were fascinated to hear about the criminal incidents, enthralled by Rolf's description of the different experts who were searching for the villains, and encouraged by his confidence there would be a satisfactory conclusion to their mission.

At the same moment, a more sinister meeting took place in the mountains within a secret lodge hidden deeply in the forest. Colonel Tarrant, Hannah Gerber, Johann Albrecht, and Gaston Bleriot had been bellowed at via teleconference by Milton Adams because of their silly attacks on a fire station and a group of tourists without any connection to Rolf Brenner's business. Worse than that, they were castigated about their idiotic assassination of some local Indians and warned about the Cherokees' inevitable revenge. Then Adams, who was at his secret headquarters in Northern Italy, shouted and issued precise instructions by laying down the law and threatening mayhem unless serious damage was inflicted on Rolf Brenner, his organisation, and the conference in Boulder.

"So there we have it," said Tarrant. "Hannah and gentlemen, chapter and verse from the Master. High time that you, Gerber, and I took full charge of this sorry group of complete amateurs, with the brilliant exception of our sharp-shooting Swiss Miss."

Tarrant and Gerber spent an hour exploring the best way to follow Milton Adams's directions and then briefed the rest of their group, which now included seven additional fighters recruited from some of the remaining Cockney Demons.

Colonel Tarrant stood at the head of the table with Hannah Gerber, now dressed in military fatigues and wearing a black beret. "Listen up, team," announced Tarrant, "Major Gerber and I will now present to you our master plan to severely damage Rolf Brenner's empire. So let's go for it, and shout, 'Hail Milton Adams,'" upon which they all cheered, and Hannah saluted.

Their first target was Belinda Carrington, Brad Coulter, and their teams, who were in their secret camp, safely hidden within the eastern part of the prairies and disguised deep in the undergrowth of the forest near a mountain lake, surrounded by rock formations. It was Maya von Gunten, the crossbow assassin, who had discovered the site of the Brenner camp, which they were now ready to attack.

Their second mission, as directed by Adams, was to follow up with an attack on Rolf Brenner's luxurious conference in the mountains. Finally, their Big Bang would be the total destruction of Brenner's conference centre in Boulder, including the staff and all the documentation about their clients, suppliers, and advisers. This would virtually destroy the credibility of RB Inc and its subsidiaries in the USA.

In the meantime, not far away, opposite to their location beyond the precarious rock formations, the chanting and drums were silenced by a commanding roar from Chief Mighty Bear, as he summoned his council to a final session in order to confirm their plans for the elimination of the murderers who had killed five of their braves and wounded several of the tribes' courageous sons and daughters.

The mighty chief decreed they would fight in the original style, adding, "Yes, take your guns, but only use them if absolutely needed. Let our trusted bows, arrows, and slings speak for us."

Tarrant and his squad had no idea they had become targets, with Cunning Fox and his sister, Little Rabbit, tracking their every move. In the meantime, Belinda had sounded an early alert just after five, as she had identified the messages of the drums and the smoke signals, based on her Cherokee background, that an attack on her initial camp was afoot. She had planned for this eventuality in detail with Brad Coulter and his agents.

Belinda's team completed preparations to leave their location but left deliberate signs of activity, such as a campfire still smouldering, the aroma of grilled meat, and the sound of splashing water from the natural spring around the corner.

"OK, troops, plan exit, so let's move," Belinda ordered.

They silently proceeded along the track, crossed the undergrowth to the other side of the valley, and then climbed to the high point above the rocky incline, where they had an excellent view of the terrain below.

Later, they noticed tell-tale movements in the undergrowth, where their adversaries silently moved closer, circled once, then crept along and made a beeline towards Belinda's original camp location about half a mile ahead.

Gerber was leading the group, and Tarrant was keeping an overview

The Molehill

of the terrain as they approached their destination; they could smell the grilled meat and the smoke from the woodfire.

"Prepare your explosives to light and hurl into the centre, then follow up with a barrage of gunfire, before storming the camp with your guns drawn," Hannah commanded. "Now go, go, go."

The sound of dynamite resounded throughout the valley, followed by several salvos of shots and then silence, as the attackers found a deserted location with some devastation by the dynamite and spent gun cartridges on the ground, resulting in plenty of swear words and much dismay, but no people.

Hannah called for silence, rallied the group, and declared, "We will now simply follow their trail. Bleriot, you and your horsemen of the Acropolis will lead the charge in the centre of our attack and make full use of the tridents you bought in Boulder. Me, I will lead the left flank and knock the stuffing out of them. Albrecht, you are in charge of the right wing and bloody well give them hell. But where the crap is von Gunten?"

Maya was indeed nowhere to be seen, having left Colorado for Italy.

Tarrant then led the way in pursuit of Belinda's group by following the trail, which had been identified by a local expert tracker who had joined their team. They made good progress until they were shocked by the powerful sounds of Indian war cries, the thundering of hooves, and the noise of invisible adversaries in the undergrowth.

They heard howls of fury as the mounted braves appeared over the horizon; those on foot emerged menacingly from the undergrowth, and then the first arrow penetrated Tarrant's chest. The French horsemen savagely clashed with the mounted warriors, speared some of their attackers with their tridents, but they were mercilessly driven back by vicious tomahawks hacking at their limbs.

Hannah immediately scooped up the severely injured Tarrant, sounded the retreat, withdrew with a sizeable contingent into the forest, and rallied them for a counterattack. As they emerged once more and started to face their adversaries, they noticed the Indians were retreating and fading away. With a shout of triumph, Gerber moved forward, urging her group to mount a savage attack.

There were no Indians left to face their attackers, but all of a sudden, a thunderous sound in addition to a powerful tremor under foot was followed by the mighty herd of buffalo sweeping over the horizon at incredible speed, trampling those who were not fast enough to flee.

Thus perished Milton's dream of destruction, which had developed into a complete and total failure. Instead of a successful mission, there were now several lost lives to mourn and quite a number of severely injured fighters to be transported to the hospital.

Rolf Brenner's conference, on the other hand, proved to be a triumph and an enormous success, after a fleet of helicopters flew the delegates to the wonderful centre near the high plains, the forest, and the mountain lake for an exhilarating time of learning, planning, and wonderful relaxation.

Chapter 25

The Termination: Switzerland and Northern Italy

Just after midnight, the little hamlet of Unterbach near the Swiss town of Meiringen was silent; everyone was asleep, and the only sounds were cowbells from the meadow nearby, an occasional dog barking, and the splashing of the Wandelbach River nearby.

Not far away, however, there was plenty of activity in one of the disguised hangars, where Colonel Peter Burki, looking ready for action and impressive in military fatigues, was briefing his commandos.

Their helicopter pilots would fly them across the snow-covered peaks, landing in the mountains of northern Italy, where they would link up with Capitano Bianca Tomassini's elite squad of Carabinieris.

The colonel, known as the Bern Bear, extended a special welcome to Sergeant Rita Liechti, Corporal Bruno Hintermann, and especially Corporal Sarah Manser who, having recovered from her serious crossbow injury, had requested to join the team and hunt down the perpetrators of the attempt on her life.

"OK, boys and girls, I have given you a heads-up of the first stage for our mission. Major Tommy Rubriger will be in command, and once we are at our destination, I will brief you about stage 2. Time to go now, team, so get your kit, total silence, and we leave at 02.00."

Soon the fleet of helicopters took off and flew along the Lauterbrunnen Valley, then branching off, following the Lutschingen

River towards Grindelwald. They climbed rapidly and flew farther until they crossed the snow-covered mountains on their way to northern Italy, where they levelled out and descended on a plateau of the Apennine Mountains. Capitano Tomassini's Carabinieris guided them to land near the mountain lake with the massive dam overlooking the steep hillside towards Bologna in the distance.

Farther down the hillside of this mountainous terrain, the modest little monastery was silent, except for the melodious tune of a single bell. The surroundings were quiet but for the gentle tinkling of the tiny bells worn by the small herd of goats, the occasional sound of a dog barking, and the eerie hoot of an owl in the giant oak tree.

At this moment, the full moon suddenly disappeared behind the massive bank of clouds, which had rolled in on time, as predicted by Peter Burki's meteorological experts. The environment was in total darkness, perfectly disguising the coordinated approach of Bianca Tomassini's Carabinieris, supported by the Swiss commandos.

Life in the monastery continued at its normal leisurely pace, with occasional songs of the choir, the sound of religious services in the middle of the night, and the regular activities of the monks on domestic duties.

This serene atmosphere of peace and quiet was in stark contrast to the turmoil down below in the secret levels below the monastery. Milton Adams was bellowing and cursing at Musgrove, his chief of staff.

"Musgrove, you slimy toad, chief of nincompoops, and a totally useless idiot, what feeble excuse have you got about the debacle in Colorado, where your favourites failed so miserably?"

"No excuses, Master. I fully share your annoyance about the devastating news, especially that the majority of our team did not survive the battle of Colorado. However, I have perfected my plan B, including all the elements you indicated are essential to secure a rapid decline of Rolf Brenner's business. My plan is complete and ready for your approval. The most important element is to secure the success of our mission.

"Leading the team and reporting to me will be Hannah Gerber, who is recovering at a private clinic in Bavaria. She will be supported by Johann Albrecht, who did exceptionally well in the mountains of Colorado. Then, my touch of genius, our devious, crafty, and invaluable Swiss Miss,

Maya von Gunten, will assist Gerber and Albrecht; she returned from the United States a few days ago. Finally for your pleasure, sir, von Gunten was allocated the suite originally occupied by her cousin, Pia Marinello, the attractive flight attendant."

"Shut up, Musgrove, waffling on about your fanciful ideas," Adams snapped. "Here are my priorities after this crazy twenty-four hours and listening to your drivel. I want you to organise a pint of Peroni then the largest grilled steak the cellarer can find, cooked rare with three fried eggs, plenty of bacon, and the best bottle of Burgundy you can find. Then you will arrange for the Swiss flight attendant to be transferred to my favourite room, ready for my special attention.

"So get it? That's my scene, Musgrove: a sumptuous, delicious feast followed by the excitement of putting that lovely Pia through my treatment, before floating her along the lake to finally disappearing into oblivion down the massive waterfall."

This was Adams's idea of a pleasurable programme. However, Peter Burki certainly had other ideas, as the colonel prepared for a final assault on the Molehill, Milton's secret headquarters of evil. Brother Enrico, Bianca's secret agent and dutiful monk at the monastery, was ready for his dangerous mission to trigger the start of spoiling Adams's evening.

As part of the young monk's plan, he was assigned to permanent service duty in the lavish suites, facilities, and personal quarters below the monastery which were securely enclosed and completely soundproof to prevent any sign of their existence to the outside world.

Enrico had cunningly ingratiated himself to Brother Anselmo by bidding to all his wishes in order to gain full freedom to all location; he then planned his move with Capitano Tomassini; they had been close friends since their early days at the county college.

As the two of them agreed, his first priority was to gain the confidence of Pia Marinello, who was enjoying a holiday with wonderful service in a lavish suite and all the facilities, delicious food, and beverages anyone could possibly wish for; however, she felt trapped in being unable to leave her location. The Swiss girl readily appreciated Enrico's cunning plan to secretly escape from this restrictive environment.

A few days earlier, Enrico had prepared another angle of his cunning plan by meeting Musgrove, who was smarting in his lavish office after another barrage from Adams.

Enrico carefully approached and said, "Mr Musgrove, sir, I am preparing for our sharp-shooting Swiss, Maya von Gunten, and her return to support your celebrated projects. It occurs to me she should be allocated Miss Marinello's premium suite; I suggest relocating Miss Pia farther along the corridor, in slightly less luxurious number 3."

And so the scene was set for the ultimate drama well below the foundations of the innocent monastery on the hillside above Bologna.

As Adams enjoyed his steak and eggs, washed down with the second bottle of the finest burgundy, Brother Enrico went into action and surreptitiously opened the door to Pia's new enclosure, number 3.

"Time to go, Miss Marinello," he whispered. "Plain clothes, no uniform, only your handbag with essentials, and complete silence, please."

Pia nodded; she was prepared, having memorized the young monk's earlier instructions.

They silently descended to the third and lowest level of this secret location, which was a service area with air-conditioning plants and all sorts of machinery. At the end of the corridor, Enrico lifted an iron cover disguised as a waste disposal unit to reveal a ladder, which led deep into the hillside. Although frightened, Pia put on a brave face as they entered the narrow rocky passage; they passed an opening which showed an enormous, powerful waterfall. Then there was another ladder to climb, which seemed to go on forever but finally revealed a wooden door, which Enrico opened.

As Pia stepped out, she was overwhelmed to be greeted by newly promoted Sergeant Sarah Manser, who smiled and said, "Welcome, Pia, if I may; you and I are going to have some fun and then whenever you wish, I will return you safely to your lovely apartment in Baden."

In the meantime, Maya von Gunten was in her dressing gown, preening herself in the mirror of her lavish suite, having enjoyed a most enjoyable spa experience. Angela, the muscular masseuse, then invited the sharp-shooting imposter to accompany her to the ultimate treatment room at one of the lower levels. Maya was amused because Angela called her Miss Pia; she followed her down two flights of stairs to the basement,

The Molehill

where an enormous door opened electronically and revealed Milton Adams, wearing a dressing gown.

"Welcome, lovely Pia Marinello," Adams said as he pulled her into a luxurious room with a double bed, but then Maya noticed the cavern behind, which included an array of ropes, chains, whips, a noose, and what looked like an electric chair. Maya screamed and tried to run away, but Angela grabbed her and tied her hands behind her back with a short length of rope.

After a moment to recover, Maya grinned and said, "Wow, Mr Adams, I admire your sense of humour, but why do you both call me Pia? You know I am her cousin Maya, your secret informer and crossbow champion, and I have delivered Pia for your amusement, my Lord." She bowed and burst into laughter.

"Come on, Angela, let's get on with it," Adams growled. "Give this nasty little liar a shot with the cattle probe." He laughed at Maya's scream as the electrical probe touched her arm.

In the meantime, Capitano Bianca Tomassini and her squad of Carabinieris had prepared the controls to partially open the gate of the dam for a brief period, which would guide the water down the waterfall, to the underground area of the monastery. On the signal from Colonel Burki, they pulled the lever and targeted the flow to thunder down the narrow gorge and into the subterranean molehill of Adams's lavish locations below the peaceful monastery.

The effect of the enormous amount of water that rushed into the subterranean levels completely snuffed out any movement, except for a black helicopter, which was seen taking off behind the turmoil; it circled a few times and then rose higher and higher, eventually disappearing into the Swiss Alps.

"Should we shoot it down?" Major Tommy Rubriger asked Colonel Burki.

"No, Tommy, whoever is escaping will continue to be on our radar."

The Carabinieris, the Swiss commandos, their commanders, and all their assistants cheered, and then they inspected the ruins that were left behind. Later, they enjoyed a lavish feast in one of Bologna's famous restaurants. The Swiss and Italian authorities complimented the colonel and capitano on a splendid conclusion, and the story went viral on the international media.

A single melodious bell at the monastery signalled the time for morning vespers; the wonderful choir prepared the world for a peaceful day of reflection and gratitude to the Lord.

Chapter 26

Breaking News: International Media

Northern Italy: Capitano Bianca Tomassini's elite squad of Carabinieris and Colonel Burki's Swiss commandos destroyed the Molehill, the headquarters of an evil organization which had grown into a sinister empire through deceit, intimidation, strong arm tactics, and murder.

Swiss National Media: Colonel Burki was invited to address the Swiss Parliament about the background, strategy, and tactics in combination with Capitano Bianca Tomassini's elite Carabinieris in destroying a serious threat to international business.

Italian Tabloids: *Bravo, bravo, bravissimo, Capitano Tomassini, Carabinieris, Colonel Burki, Swizzero commandos; the Molehill, Finito Basta.*

International Financial Media: Swiss and Italian commandos destroyed an evil company known as the Molehill; this was lauded as a shot in the arm for local business in Hampshire and Rolf Brenner's subsidiaries in UK, Germany, Switzerland, and the United States.

The *Boston Globe*: An invasion of vicious hornets has worried residents in Falmouth and in the Cape Cod area, combined with some strange business activities and unusual accidents, which appear to threaten the peace and quiet of this beautiful location. A senior scientist at Harvard expressed his concern about mysterious hornet's nests, which appear somehow to be linked to erratic human behaviour.

Wallstreet Media: Superb news for investors and the stock market with the destruction of the evil organization known as the Molehill.

About the Author

Kurt Hafner

Kurt was born, educated and trained in his native Switzerland against a family background of hospitality, teachers, authors, broadcasters, lecturers. He demonstrated plenty of creativity and imagination from an early age and is fluent in five languages. His first romanticised novel of 'Two School Boys Stalking Wildlife' was published shortly after his 16th birthday.

Thereafter Kurt focussed on his expertise in hospitality, working five seasons at the Royal Palace Hotel Gstaad, the Ritz Barcelona, eight years at The Dorchester in Park Lane, followed by 30 years as Senior Manager with global responsibilities at BOAC then British Airways.

As Chairman of a Europe wide trade association he widened his scope, became recognized as an authority in his field, contributed to publications, presented papers and lectured at universities in England, Switzerland and France.

After retirement from British Airways Kurt was retained as a consultant and ran his business from his home in leafy Hampshire, where he provides a specialist service to premium clients.

Kurt's first International dramatic thriller 'Spider's Web' was published several years ago and is now followed by a sequel 'The Molehill' as a prelude to his future novels 'The Hornet's Nest' and 'The Wolves Lair'.

Kurt and his wife Mary have been married for over sixty years, enjoy the company of their dogs and take great delight in their three daughters and their families who all live nearby.